TERRITORY TYRANNY

ROCKY MOUNTAIN SAINT BOOK 11

B.N. RUNDELL

WOLFPACK PUBLISHING
— EST 2013 —

Territory Tyranny

Paperback Edition
© Copyright 2019 B.N. Rundell

Wolfpack Publishing
6032 Wheat Penny Avenue
Las Vegas, NV 89122

wolfpackpublishing.com

Paperback ISBN 978-1-64119-570-6
eBook ISBN 978-1-64119-569-0

Library of Congress Control Number: 2019936124

Secrets . . . *everbody's got 'em. And because they're secrets, we
don't often share them.*
*Unless you're a writer. Then your writing is infused with secrets
that are secretly hidden and secretly shared. Sometimes there
are those that can uncover and recognize those secrets, and the
special people smile, enjoy and never share them. That's why
special people should always be treasured and appreciated. I
have a long list of special people which of course begins with my
precious wife. But that list continues with my publisher, Mike
Bray, and his right hand that he would be helpless without,
Rachel Del Grosso. These two read most, I think, but not all of
what I write and probably get a few laughs along the way. Then
there's Aubrey, my editor, who, when she reads my work, she
probably gets headaches and moans and groans at my snide
remarks, but she perseveres. And writing would be a colossal
waste of time without readers. Readers that step into your imag-
ination, hang on, and see it through, only to pick up another one
and try again, hoping for something better each time.
Thank you one and all. The only people I share my secrets with!*

TERRITORY TYRANNY

CHAPTER ONE
WAR

"WOULD YOU LOOK AT THAT!? THEY MUSTA GOT A MIGHTY early start, ya' reckon?" asked Sean. Tate and his son, Sean, sat, leaning on the pommels of their saddles as their horses shifted their weight from one leg to the other, almost in unison. They were atop a finger ridge that over-looked the North Platte River and the Oregon Trail. The long line of white-bonneted wagons had started circling for their night's camp, a familiar sight to the two observers. They had guided other wagon trains and helped several more and knew enough about the trail they now followed, to know the settlers had their work and trials ahead.

"They had to start out at the first sign of spring back in Missouri, sometime in March, probably. Maybe they brought spring with 'em," chuckled Tate, twisting around in his seat to lift his face to the warm sun. "The way that sun's shinin', that mountain snow's gonna be meltin' an' the rivers are gonna be risin' soon!"

"Ma always liked spring best. Lookee there," Sean

pointed to a cluster of Chiming Bells showing their first blooms of purple, "and there," pointing to another small patch of Blue Flax. "Those are some of her favorites!"

"You're right about that. Course, dependin' on where we were or the time of year, her favorites changed with the seasons. She likes 'em all!"

"Ya think we oughta go say our hellos?" asked Sean, hopefully. Since their friends, the Bottineau's, had returned to their homes in the far north, neither had the opportunity to have a conversation with anyone other than themselves since last summer. Sean had been despondent for more than a month after their friends left. The family had stayed almost a year with them in the Wind River Mountains and Sean and their daughter, Reindeer Fawn, had become quite close. They were best friends, and both thought their friendship might become even more, but her mother, Red Leaf, wanted to return to her people, the Santee Dakota. Now, Sean was hopeful of at least meeting someone new, someone to talk to besides his father.

Sean was the spitting image of his father, although just pushing sixteen, he was what most would call a full-grown man. Standing just shy of six feet, broad-shoul-dered, a lean frame that tapered to narrow hips, and wavy brown hair that curled over the collar of his buckskin tunic. The only life he had known was the mountains, and his only friends, other than Fawn, were Indians. They had lived near the Arapaho in the Wind Rivers, and when they lived in the Sangre De Cristo's, they were near the Ute and the Comanche. They had close friends among all these tribes, and both Sean, and his father spoke most of the languages fluently; and were skilled with sign language used by all the tribes.

They were making their spring supply trip to Fort Laramie and Fort Bernard, following the Oregon Trail. Since the snow in the Laramie Mountains was still too deep to cross the shorter route that they usually traveled, they now sat on their promontory observing the wagons below. Without speaking, Tate gigged his grulla, Shady, forward to start their descent toward the wagons. Both men led pack-horses, although the packs were empty in anticipation of their buying trip, the fresh-killed carcass of a mule deer hung across one. Sean straddled his Appaloosa, Dusty, so named because of the coloring across his rump that looked like dust on a white blanket. They rocked back and forth in their saddles as the horses picked their way down the slope, an occasional grunt and the creak of the leather accompanied the percussion symphony of hooves kicking rocks aside.

Tate breathed deep, taking in the pungent aroma of sagebrush and greasewood. Father and son leaned back, shifting their weight to the rear of their horses, giving the animals more stability as they often slid on the steep descent of the loose gravel trail. When they bottomed out, each man sat upright, looking to the wagons. As they neared, Tate called out, "Haloo the camp!"

His shout had startled those nearest to their approach, and they watched as men scrambled to the wagons for their rifles and women grabbed at the youngsters to hide them behind the wagons. Tate chuckled and with one hand held high, "We're friendly, just stoppin' to say hello!"

"Come ahead on, keep your hands away from them rifles!" came an order from a man that stood behind a wagon box. All that showed was a floppy felt hat, a whiskered face, and a red bulbous nose.

Tate nodded to Sean, and the two rode closer to the wagon. Tate saw the man's eyes grow large when he looked beside the horses and saw a big grey wolf beside Shady and a sizable black wolf beside Dusty. "They're friendly too, but they are protective," declared Tate. "S'alright we get down?"

"Sure, sure. Just as soon as you tell us why you're out here in the middle of nowhere," instructed the speaker, still partially obscured behind the wagon and pointing his rifle towards the visitors.

"First of all, my friend, we're not in the middle of nowhere. This is my country, and you're the visitors. But, since you're new to this country and haven't learned the ways of the west, we, my son and I, are on our way to Fort Bernard to resupply. I'm Tate, and this is my son, Sean," answered Tate, leaning his arms on the pommel of his saddle as he looked at the cautious man.

"Well, then, I s'pose it'd be alright for you to get down," said the speaker as he stepped out from behind the wagon. "I'm Fergis Morgan, and we're headin' to South Pass and on to Oregon!"

Tate and Sean swung down from their horses, Tate handing the reins to Sean as he asked, "Could you folks use some fresh meat?"

A wide smile split Fergis' face, "Boy howdy! We ain't had fresh meat since the other side o' Laramie!" He turned to a woman behind the wagon, "C'mon Ma, let's get us some meat." A portly woman clad in homespun came from behind the wagon, red cheeks and nose framing a wide smile. Her eyes sparkled with a hint of mischief as she grabbed a pan from the wagon.

"No need for the pan, ma'am. You folks can have the whole deer, that is, if you share it with the others," nodded Tate as he looked to see other people coming from behind the wagons.

Tate and Sean were suddenly the objects of most of the settlers' attention as they walked up and extended hands to shake as they introduced themselves. Tate dragged the deer carcass from the packhorse and dropped it to the ground, "There ya go folks, I'm sure Mr. Morgan will be glad to share."

As they watched the families divvy up the meat, two riders approached, and from atop their mounts, they looked at Tate and Sean, and one asked, "And who might you be?"

Tate immediately detected an attitude coming from the man and thought he might be either the wagonmaster or scout but chose to be careful in his answer anyway. "Who's askin'?" replied Tate, turning to look at the man. What he saw was a weathered face with a mustache that drooped below the corners of a stern mouth. Dark brown hair carried a splash of grey over his ears, a wide-brimmed felt hat shaded black eyes that scowled from under bushy brows. He was a big man made all the bigger as he sat on a rawboned horse that looked meaner than a mistreated mule. The man scowled, leaned forward on his pommel and growled, "I'm the wagonmaster, mister, now answer my question or git!"

Tate held the man's gaze for a moment, then reached for Shady's reins, turned the horses to put the animals between them and the questioner, and both father and son stepped into their stirrups and swung aboard. As they hit their saddles, both men had pushed their jackets open and had their hands resting on the butts of their pistols.

As Tate started to leave, Morgan stepped forward, "Now hold on there! Jake, this man has given us a whole deer and that ain't no way to treat 'em! 'Sides, he already told us his name was Tate and the other'ns Sean, they're father an' son. And we was gonna ask 'em to supper!"

The wagonmaster turned to look at Morgan, then at the carcass that others were still busy stripping, and back at Tate. "You did that?"

Tate just looked at the man, nodding slightly, but saying nothing.

The wagon master looked at Tate, back to Morgan, and then he shook his head like he remembered something. He lifted his eyes to Tate and extended his hand, "I'm Jake Wilkins," then turned to indicate the other rider, "And this is Rocky Rhodes, my scout."

Tate moved Shady alongside the wagonmaster's horse and shook hands with the man. As Jake held Tate's hand, he asked, "Did you say your name is Tate?"

"That's right."

"Would it be Tate Saint?"

Tate frowned and answered, "That's right."

"Then you must be the man General Harney called the Rocky Mountain Saint, is that right?"

"I've been called that, yes."

By now, the scowling wagonmaster's expression had softened to a semblance of a smile, and he continued, "The General hoped we might run into you, and he said if we did to let you know he'd like you to come to the fort. He acted like he had something special for you." Before

Tate could respond, Jake looked around and motioned for them to dismount.

The four men walked together to the nearby riverbank where the mountain men would make their camp and tether their horses. Jake spoke, "Sorry 'bout bein' so unfriendly before, but we've had more'n our share of trouble, and I guess we're just a little spooky."

"Indians?" asked Tate.

"Oh, we saw some Pawnee, Kiowa, maybe some Sioux, but none came near or gave us any trouble. But we had some trouble with white men. Seems ever'body's tense an' wantin' to fight what with what's goin' on back east. Just makes us more anxious to get to Oregon an' away from all that."

Tate looked at the man, "Wha's goin' on back east?"

"Oh, it's that same ol' argument 'bout slavery. Some wants it, others don't, and they can't agree on anything. Now, it looks like it's gonna be war."

"War? Whad'dya mean, war?"

They stopped walking as Jake looked to Tate, "We didn't hear 'bout it till we got to Fort Kearny, but the Confederates attacked Fort Sumpter and now it 'pears there's gonna be an all-out war!"

"Are they crazy?" asked an incredulous Tate, shaking his head, unbelieving.

"I think so, but when you got politicians in charge, what else can you expect?"

"Well, sounds like somebody's gonna have to explain a few things to this mountain man. Where's Fort Sumpter and what's Confederates?"

CHAPTER TWO
CONTEMPLATION

Mrs. Morgan sat a fine table, showing no regard for their location on the cactus flats beside the North Platte River, hundreds of miles from any semblance of civilization. She loved to entertain and had spread a colorful table cloth and gathered a handful of flowers to decorate the table. She assigned the seats for Tate, Sean, and Jake, but put her husband at the head of the table, seating herself and their daughter, Melissa, to his right. Fergis asked the Lord's blessing on their bounty and at the "Amen," everyone anxiously lifted their heads to begin the feast.

The venison steaks had been battered, breaded and fried while a small wash basin was used for the milk gravy, made possible by the milk cow they had brought all the way from Missouri. She had fried some thin-sliced Indian potatoes and fixed a medley of Prickly Pear hips, cat-tail root, and dehydrated sweet potatoes that was surprisingly tasty.

"Mrs. Morgan, I must say, we haven't eaten this well

for a long time! This is all delicious!" declared Tate, between mouthfuls.

"Thank you, Mr. Saint, you're very kind," answered the smiling and pleased woman. "And we are very thankful for the fresh meat you provided."

The small talk continued until after everyone had their fill and topped it off with a slice of wild rhubarb pie. The men sat back, some lighting pipes, all holding steaming cups of coffee. Tate looked to the wagonmaster, "So, how 'bout fillin' me in on all the happenings back east."

As Jake began, several leaned forward to listen carefully, "Well, after the Republicans put Lincoln in office, it seemed that the pot just began to boil. Before that, several of the southerners started talking secession, Lincoln tried to appease them and keep the nation together, but the issue of slavery and states' rights just couldn't be settled. So, several, I think seven or eight, I'm not sure, of the southern states, banded together to secede and form what they called a Confederacy. I don't know all the details, but it also divided the military, and the southern men formed their own army. Even got some of the officers an' generals to join 'em, and then they decided to attack Fort Sumpter. See, it was a federal fort, but it was in South Carolina, near Charleston, and South Carolina had seceded and was part of the Confederacy. General Beauregard was in command, and when the Union tried to reinforce the fort, the Confederates attacked and took the fort. So, last I heard, what we found out at Fort Kearney as we come through, Lincoln was asking for 75,000 men to quell what he called the rebellion. So, it seems like there's a big ol' war that done started up. Some apparently think it won't last but a few months, but they been arguing about it longer than that, so . . . " he shrugged his shoulders and looked at the others.

Most just sat, shaking their heads, wondering what was going to happen. Tate lifted his eyes to Jake Wilkins, "What about Missouri?"

"They haven't seceded, but there's folks on both sides of the argument, same as in Kentucky. I guess only time will tell."

Tate was thinking about his wife, Maggie, and their daughter, Sadie. When Sadie wanted to have a regular education and to live away from the mountains, Maggie agreed to take her to St. Louis and stay with the child through that time. They were with Tate's Aunt LaVinia Finney at her boarding house and Inn, and the rumors of war gave Tate considerable concern. He unconsciously patted his chest pocket that held the last three letters from his wife, and two letters from him that would be mailed at Fort Laramie. He breathed deep and looked at his son, who was staring at the flames, probably wondering about the same things.

To change the subject, Jake looked to Tate and asked, "Should we be concerned about Indians between here'n South Pass?"

"Haven't you been through here before?" inquired Tate, shaking his head at the presumption of the man.

"Yeah, I have, but it's been quite a few years back. I only took on this job 'cause the first wagonmaster we had got stumble down drunk, fell in the river and got snake-bit by a water moccasin and panicked and drowned. That was back near the Missouri/Kansas border and what with all the Redlegs an' such, we decided to keep on goin'."

Tate and Sean exchanged incredulous looks, then Tate

said, "Mister, from here to Oregon, you better keep a sharp eye out and your powder dry, 'cause you're liable to see hostiles anywhere and ever'where!"

All those nearby that heard his warning stopped and looked at the buckskin-clad mountain men and waited for more. "Why, summer 'fore last, we guided some pilgrims on a buffalo hunt, went up that trail you passed right back yonder, and we was attacked by a big band of Brulé Sioux. Lost a few men, had a woman captured, all-in-all a rather unpleasant experience. And from here on out, there's gonna be more of the same. Right now, you're sittin' between Sioux territory and Crow territory, least-ways that's what the Treaty of '51 says, an' further on you'll be cuttin' Arapaho territory, then you'll get into Ute country, and Piute," he paused shaking his head. "And I bet you ain't got any look-outs posted tonight either, have you?"

"Uh, no, we don't. Should we?"

Tate looked at the man and shook his head, "Only if you don't wanna get all these folks scalped in their sleep. Jake, you're followin' the Platte to the Sweetwater, and right about there you'll see a mass grave. There were twenty wagons of folks, just like this bunch, and we had to bury ever'one of 'em. The Cheyenne and Crow had banded together, took 'em by surprise, and didn't leave a livin' soul behind."

Silence fell over the group; no one moved as they looked at the visitors, and when Tate stood, others moved from their seats or from where they stood, and Tate continued, "You should have guards that move around all night long, always watching, ready to give the alarm. If there's folks that don't know how to shoot, women and men, teach 'em. I know you folks never expected this to be a stroll in the park, but you also need to know that the trail from here to Oregon is long and hard. Many of you won't make it, and you'll pass the graves of hundreds of others just like you. But it can be done, if you work together and you make ready to face anything that comes at you. And if it was me, I wouldn't move until I had some time in prayer, maybe together, and committed each day to the Lord."

After a few moments, Jake looked to Tate again, "Would you consider leadin' us at least to South Pass?"

Tate shook his head, "No, I've got to see General Harney at Fort Laramie, remember? And we have other obligations. You'll do fine, Jake, just use your common sense and be watchful."

Father and son stood, and both men shook hands with those nearby, extended their thanks to Mrs. Morgan for the fine meal, and excused themselves to return to their camp by the river. Once alone, Sean asked, "Pa, you worried 'bout Ma?"

They had checked on the horses, and satisfied, were now laying out the bedrolls and Tate stopped, looked at his son, "Yeah, Sean, I am. Well, maybe not worried, but at least concerned. You remember what it was like back in St. Louis and the conversations we've had about slaves and such. It's a difficult issue. Some folks have been so accustomed to having slaves, and they built their farms with slave labor. While others chose not to be a part of that and now stand against it. So, when you have folks of both beliefs in close proximity, you're going to have conflict, and that's what I'm concerned about. It's too easy for others to fight and argue while innocent folks get caught in the crossfire."

"You don't really think Ma and Sadie are in danger now, do you?"

"That's just it; I don't know."

"So, what're we gonna do?"

"Well, I figger we'll wait till we get to Ft. Laramie, see if we got any letters from Ma and what she says. Then we'll see what General Harney wants, and we'll trust the Lord to guide us."

Sean sat down on the bedroll, thoughtful as he started to crawl in the blankets, and said, "Pa, I don't wanna go to St. Louis."

Tate looked at his son, "Might not have to, but what if they need help?"

"You can handle it, whatever it might be, but I'd rather stay here. I had my fill of things when we took Sadie and Ma back there, and I just can't stand the idea of goin' back."

"But, if I have to go, you'll be alone."

"Yeah, I thought about that. But you came west all alone, and you were younger'n I am now."

"Yeah, I was," answered Tate as they both crawled into their bed-covers. It was a clear night, and the milky way paved its way across the heavens, leaving the myriad of stars twinkling in the darkness, beckoning thoughts from the two men that lay side-by-side, hands clasped behind their heads as they searched the stars for answers.

CHAPTER THREE
CONSIDERATION

IT WAS MID-AFTERNOON WHEN TATE AND SEAN RODE
through the gate of Fort Laramie. They had planned on
re-supplying at the nearby Fort Bernard because Laramie
had become more of an army post, but since General
Harney had passed word that he wanted to see Tate, they
chose to stop in and visit with the commandant. They
tethered their horses at the Sutler's, loosening their
cinches to give them a well-earned breather, and walked
to the Headquarters room. The men were readily ushered
into the General's office and greeted warmly.

"Tate! Sean! Good to see you two! I certainly didn't
think you'd be here so soon."

"General," nodded Tate as the men shook hands. At the
commandant's motion, father and son were seated before
the general's desk as he dropped into his high-backed
chair and leaned back, hands clasped across his ample
belly.

"So, have you heard the news?" asked the grinning
uniformed man.

"Well, we heard some from a wagonmaster we met last night. Just about the attack on Sumpter and the president's call for troops. Doesn't sound too good," answered Tate, leaning forward slightly, anxious to hear more.

"My news is close to a week old, but now they've got this new-fangled invention called the telegraph to Fort Kearney, and they're thinkin' it'll be here by the end of the year. Anyway, things have been movin' mighty fast, on both the Confederate and Union sides. Sounds like this is gonna be an all-out war like this country's never seen before. I received orders to march to Jefferson Barracks in St. Louis and take the Second Dragoons and two companies of the mounted infantry. That leaves a skeleton crew here to man the fort under Captain Steele."

"This place is gonna look like a ghost town!" declared Tate, looking around as if he could see the cobwebs already.

"Ummhumm, but we have to keep it manned. I don't really think there'll be any problems with the Sioux, at least I hope not, after the lesson I taught 'em at Ash Hollow."

"That was what, four, five years ago? And that certainly didn't stop that bunch of Brulé from attacking us a couple summers ago!" replied Tate. "But what does that all have to do with us, General?"

The general leaned forward, putting his elbows on his desk, looking very stern, "I need you to be our scout and guide back to St. Louis."

"What do you need a guide for? Just follow the rivers; they'll get you there."

The general leaned back, grinning, "If it was only that easy. We got word from Kearney that the Sioux, Pawnee, and Kiowa are all causing problems, and that's not even mentioning the rabble called Red Legs and Jayhawkers in Kansas! My orders are to get my command there, intact! And we have to be ready to be assigned into the war as soon as we get there! I can't do it if I lose men to Indians and troublemakers!" He pounded his fist on his desk to emphasize his point, making the stack of papers on the corner bounce and fall in a mess. He stood and walked to the corner of the desk nearest Tate, "I need you to scout ahead and keep us out of trouble, and it's only a man with your experience and savvy that can do it!"

"What about my son?" asked Tate in a calm voice that mellowed the mood in the office. The general went back to his chair and plopped down, "That's why I wanted you both here." He looked at Sean, "The word I have is you know as much about the Indians as your pa and that you're just as knowledgeable about the country and mountains as your pa, is that right?"

Sean shifted nervously in his seat, looked at his pa and back at the General, "Well, General, I reckon I know more than most men about the native peoples, I speak most of their languages and sign language as well, and I know considerable about the country roundabouts, but," he dropped his head, smiling, and grinned at his pa, "I don't think I'll ever know as much as pa."

"Good answer, son," said Tate, laughing with his son.

The general chuckled, nodding his head, "Yes, good answer. But here's what I need of you. Captain Steele will be left in command, but," and he leaned to look around Tate to the door to ensure it was closed, "between us, I believe that he will be leaving soon. Oh, he won't get orders, but what's happening all over, is those that have

Southern sympathies are just up and leaving to join up with the Confederates. Now, that's just part of it." He looked to Tate, "Did you ever meet the Indian Agent for the Sioux, Thomas Twiss?"

"No, sir, never did. Heard of him, though."

He addressed himself to both Tate and Sean and began to explain, "He's been a thorn in my side ever since he came out here. He interfered when I wanted to talk peace with the Oglalas and told them to stay away. Well, I got him fired as agent, but his family had connections back east, and he got himself restored. And he's been more of an Indian than a white man, took him a squaw even though he's got himself a wife back east. He graduated from West Point, second in his class!" He paused in his comments, shook his head and lifted his face to the men, grinning, "But Lincoln had him removed! Finally! It's been thought he was skimming off the top whenever the annuities came, and now with the war, their annuity didn't include the usual powder and lead; he might cause problems."

He looked to Sean, "I need you to scout around, that's all, to try to keep an eye on things and any possible problems with the Sioux, and anyone else for that matter. The army tells me they will send some volunteer companies out to man the fort, eventually. But, with so few here, and maybe even some of them switching sides and deserting, there's no tellin' what might happen. But it would be good if there was somebody around when the new outfits get here to kind of teach 'em the ropes, if you know what I mean?"

"Are there any 'boundaries' regarding what I should do, or just use my own judgment?" asked Sean, prompting a surprised Tate to lean back and look at his son, this man that just asked this question and offered to make his own decisions.

"Just like you said, use your own discernment. I think you know how to stay out of trouble and since you won't be in any 'official' capacity, no one can try to tell you what to do. Although you will be drawing full Scout's pay! And it might be that, after the other troops are stationed here, the new commandant will be smart enough to take advantage of your experience and keep you on full pay." ·

Sean grinned at the words 'full pay' and looked to Tate to see a grinning and very proud father. The three men shook hands on the agreement, and Tate asked, "How soon we leaving?"

"Now that you're here, tomorrow morning soon enough?" asked Harney.

"Soon enough."

Both men were silent as they walked side by side back to the Sutler. Tate turned to Sean, "Let's get supplied; then we'll make camp down by the river." Sean nodded in agreement as the two walked into the supply center. Their order differed now, with the men going separate ways, but they thought about each need and stacked goods accordingly. Tate settled up as Sean started packing stuff outside, and within a short while, both pack horses were loaded, and they left the fort to make a camp in the trees by the river. As they passed through the gate, they paid little attention to the usual double takes they received. The men were almost mirror images of one another, even to each having a wolf trotting alongside; they were impressive and memorable figures of a slowly disappearing west.

. . .

"So, Pa, ya think you'll be bringin' Ma and Sadie back home?" asked Sean as he stirred the strips of pork belly among the beans in the pan. He was sitting on the big end of a downed cottonwood that put him on the level of the pot that hung suspended over the fire.

"Well, I dunno. If there's not any danger, they'll probably want to stay there so Sadie can stay in school. But, war changes everything. So . . . " and he let the thought hang in the air between them, giving each a brief opportunity to think on the unresolved subject for a moment or two. Blank stares into the flames showed thoughtful men with shared burdens.

"You think the war will reach out here?" asked Sean.

"I think the only war that reaches out here will be with the Indians. And I'm pretty sure the natives wouldn't mind if all the white men shot each other and left them alone!"

"You're probably right about that."

"So, tell me, son, *in your own judgment*, just what are you going to do?"

Sean couldn't help but laugh at his pa's emphasis on the judgment part, but then he looked at the pot and back at his pa. "I think I'll just take my time, kinda mosey around, do a thorough scout of the Oglala and the Brulé, maybe the Miniconjou, and just see what they're up to. And, like you taught me, I figger on doin' most of that at night."

Tate dropped his head, poked at a couple of red and black ants with a stick, then looked up to Sean, "That's pretty good judgment, son. And, I know what you said to the general, but I've taught you, watched you, and you are every bit as knowledgeable about the country and the natives as I am. And in the woods, I think you're even better than I am. And you know how to use your longbow as well as I can, and you can shoot even better. I'm mighty proud of you, son."

Sean dropped his eyes; he didn't want to have his pa see the water that came up in them and breathed a deep breath before he could look up. "All I ever wanted to be was just like you, Pa."

"All I ever wanted, was for you to be better than me, son."

TATE TWISTED AROUND IN HIS SADDLE TO TAKE ONE LAST look at his son, standing by the main gate of Fort Laramie and watching the long line of blue snake its way to the deep rutted Oregon Trail as it pointed southeast. Neither man lifted his hand, but both knew the other watched. As the shuffling gait of the hundreds of horses and six wagons stirred up the dry alkali laden dust, the men at the head of the line; General Harney, Colonel Philip Cooke, Captain Beverly Robertson and their scout, Tate, soon disappeared in the pale brown cloud. Sean dropped his eyes to the ground, turned back into the fort and made his way to the headquarters building. Captain Steele stood under the overhang, and Sean asked, "Did the General leave some paperwork for me to look over?"

"Hummph, yes, he did. And I don't understand why someone that's still wet behind the ears should have access to the treaties and other information that should only be for the eyes of officers in the military!" growled the pompous captain.

Sean just looked at the man without responding, keeping his expression somber, and waited for him to provide the requested information. After a few tense moments, the captain pushed away from the post he had used to lean on, and turned back into the office. Sean followed, and the captain directed him to a stack of papers on the corner of the orderly's desk. Sean looked at the stack, back at the captain, and started to reach for the papers, when Steele said, "And don't you take those from this office. You can use that table by the window and when you're done, give every one of those to the orderly!"

Sean slowly lifted his head to nod, turned away from the obstinate officer and picked up the stack to take them to the table. He seated himself and began his study. Before him were the documents of the 1851 Treaty of Laramie or the Horse Creek Treaty as it was known by the tribes. There was also the proposed treaty submitted by Thomas Twiss, which was rejected by the government, and a scrawled list of engagements between the tribes and with settlers and soldiers. Sean had asked for the information to better understand both sides and the boundaries that had been accepted by the different people.

As he read, Sean remembered the times he and his pa had talked about the treaty. It had been the first widespread comprehensive attempt at bringing peace to the great plains. Tate had explained about the different territories for each of the tribes and the promises of the whites to provide payment in the form of annuities of supplies and provisions, most of which were never paid. "The tribes to the south, the Comanche, Kiowa, and Apache, wouldn't come up and sign the treaty because Fort

Laramie is in Sioux territory. Can't blame 'em; they been enemies for as long as any of 'em can remember."

"But who broke the treaty first, pa?" asked Sean as they sat on the porch of their cabin. Sean was a youngster, in his early teen years, and it was a pretty complex subject to explain to the curious boy.

"From what I hear, the tribes didn't like the idea of being told where they could and could not hunt, and the way they tell it, the Sioux fought against the Crow and the Cheyenne and anybody else that was in their way. Then the white man, who was supposed to have safe passage across their territory, decided to try to settle down or go lookin' for gold, and then they got into it with just about ever' one of the tribes as they crossed the country. You know the Oregon Trail, we've traveled it, and it goes through Sioux, Crow, Arapaho, Cheyenne, and Ute territory. Just too many people and too many wagons for the Indians."

As Sean remembered the conversation, he looked at the map drawn by Father DeSmet, the Catholic mission priest to the Indians, and he recognized the different territories. When he read the proposed treaty from the Indian Agent Thomas Twiss, he saw, *Oglala to live on Horse and Deer Creek, Brulés on the White River east of the Black Hills, the Cheyennes on Laramie Creek and Arapahos on the Cache la Poudre River.* Sean thought of those areas, knowing each one and having hunted or traveled in all that country.

He turned his attention to the list of conflicts between the tribes and with white settlers and soldiers. Most had been minor encounters with few fatalities, and were usually retaliatory actions for some confrontation, often caused by a misunderstanding. Such as the Battle of Ash Hollow that had been led by General Harney and was an escalation after the Grattan Massacre which was the fault of an over-eager green lieutenant. All mistakes that led to the deaths of almost a hundred Sioux and thirty soldiers. Sean sat and shook his head at the arrogance and pride, that was the root of the problem.

After two hours of close scrutiny of the paperwork, he shuffled the stack together, handed it to the orderly, and left without speaking. His horses were still tethered by the river, with ample graze and access to water, and watched over by the big black wolf, Indy. As Sean walked from the fort, he carefully considered what he believed to be the most important part of his mission; to reconnoiter the different bands of the Sioux and if time and opportunity allowed, to at least see where the other bands were gathered and what they were doing.

He checked on Dusty and the packhorse, the dapple-grey gelding that had served so well as a pack animal and spare mount. They had grazed down the grass within reach of their tether, and he pulled the stake and moved the two near a good bunch of tall green. Indy was at his heels, and he talked to the wolf, "Well boy, looks like its just gonna be us for a while. You're gonna have to do your best and keep a good watch out for us. But right now, how 'bout we get us some o' that stew from last night, and then get some more sleep. We'll be travelin' at night from here on out, most of the time anyway."

The big wolf poked his nose between Sean's hip and his dangling hand, seeking some attention and Sean obliged as they walked back to the smoldering coals. He pushed the pot onto the grey cinders, added a few small sticks and sat down to watch the coals bring the flames to life as they licked at the fresh fuel. He added some water to the coffee pot, and when it started brewing, he dropped in some more grounds and waited for it to boil. After a few minutes, he pulled the pot aside, put just a little cold water in to settle the grounds, and poured himself a cup of 'thinking brew.'

He began reviewing his gear. His Sharps, which had been his ma's, he kept on the packhorse, but the Spencer repeater was in the scabbard on his saddle. On the opposite side, his longbow, the one he and his pa made over the winter with the yew wood they brought from Missouri, was in its sheath under the left fender of the saddle. The quiver of arrows hung from the straps beside his cantle. He always carried his Colt Army with two extra loaded cylinders in the holster on his left hip, butt forward, on his belt, while under his right arm, the metal-bladed tomahawk hung from his braided leather belt. The big Bowie knife hung in its scabbard between his shoulder blades, handle up and easily accessible over his shoulder. He had ample ammunition and powder and shot for all his weapons in his saddle-bags and more in the packs. He had an extra set of buckskins in the packs, blankets for his bedroll, and essential food and some trade goods in the packs as well. Tate had given him some gold coin that he kept in small pockets on the inside of his belt, and he had told him of the location of the Spanish gold in the cave behind their cabin in the Sangre de Cristos.

With his gear checklist settled, he turned his thoughts to the coming journey. With the Sioux territory to the north of the fort, he planned to search for the different

Brulé camps first. With the Oglala farther north and somewhat east and the Miniconjou closer to the Black Hills, he would take each day as it came, but for now, food and rest. Tonight, would have the promise of a coming full moon, and he was anxious to take to the trail.

CHAPTER FIVE
MUSKRAT

Dusk had settled across the flats when Indy lay his head down on Sean's shoulder to nudge him awake. Sean had drifted in and out of sleep as he struggled to adjust to what his new schedule would be, travel at night and sleep during daylight. He was anxious to get started on this new chapter of his life, but he knew he had to pace himself and be constantly vigilant and cautious. There would be no one to bail him out of any trouble he might stumble into, and as his pa had always taught him, "It's best to be careful than sorry. You might not get another chance to make a mistake."

He rolled off his blankets; it had been too warm to cover up and began rolling up his bedroll. He pushed the coffee-pot into the coals, dropped a stubby stick on the ashes, and turned to gear up the horses. As the western hills cradled the sun, Sean was mounted and started toward the northern flats. He would keep the hills that had become known as the Wildcats off his left shoulder where they would provide the broken silhouette to guide his trek. He remembered his pa telling how his grandfather had taught him about the constellations and how to find the north star. "First, ya find Ursa Major, or as some call it, the Great Bear. 'Course there's other's that call it the Plough or the Wagon. But when ya' find it, it does look more like a plough than a bear, those two stars at the end of the plough, they point to Ursa Minor, or the little constellation that's just like the big one, only smaller, of course. The star at the end of the little one, that's the North star!"

Sean smiled at the memory of him and his pa standing in the clearing of their cabin in the Sangre de Cristo's and looking up at the myriad of stars as he pointed out the different constellations. It was one of those special learning times at the side of his father, a memory that would guide him in his adult years.

This was also the first time that Indy was without Lobo and the big wolf moved almost hesitantly, often looking back as if in hopes of seeing his lifelong companion. But Indy was full-grown, and even bigger than Lobo, and in the darkness, Sean thought his eyes almost blazed orange, giving the animal an ominous appearance. But Indy and Sean had grown inseparable, especially after Sadie turned her eyes to the city. Although she and the wolf were childhood companions, the relationship between Sean and Indy had become even closer in the past almost two years since they returned from St. Louis. With a wave of his hand, Sean sent the wolf forward, and big black beast took to his long lope to scout the trail ahead.

With the shadowy mountains to his left and the slow-rising moon to his right, they settled in to the anticipated night travel. As his eyes adjusted to the dim light provided by the stars and the moon waxing full, Sean began to savor the quiet of the night. The common sounds were the muted steps of the horses in the powdery alkali and sandy soil, the creak of the saddle, and the occasional drawn-out peets of the nighthawk. Cicadas rattled their ratcheting across the flats, and whenever they neared one of the few meandering run-off creeks, he would often hear the owls questioning the darkness. And of course, the lovelorn cries of the lonesome coyotes added to the chorus of the prairie.

Sean rocked to the gait of his long-legged Appaloosa, rested his elbows on the flat-topped saddle horn and let his eyes learn the shadowy shapes before them. The skeletal cholla stood like bony fingers, while the flat-bladed prickly pear showed only as dark, irregular clumps. Clusters of buffalo grass waved in the slight breeze like wispy apparitions, while sagebrush and greasewood appeared like black rocks beside the chosen trail.

This was a desolate land devoid of trees except the juniper and piñon that clung to the few ridges and hill-sides, offering little shade and less protection. The land had been formed by the winds of winter and runoffs of spring in eons past, but all had been shaped by the hands of the Creator who saw beauty in every differing land-scape. Sean loved the timbered mountains best, but he had come to enjoy and appreciate the prairies and plains and contrasting beauty of the wide-open spaces.

At every creek that offered water and graze, Sean had paused to give the animals rest and to stretch his legs as he munched on pemmican and jerky before putting his face in the cold water to drink deep and keep his senses alert. The moon was dropping past its zenith when Indy trotted back to greet Sean. As they met, Sean stepped down to run his hands through the scruff of Indy's neck and ask, "So, what'd you find, boy? Somethin' interesting?"

The wolf gave Sean an eager look, mouth open, tongue lolling, and tail swishing excitedly. Sean knew this was not the wolf's warning of danger, but rather of a discovery that might prove interesting. "Alright boy, lead on!" instructed Sean as he swung back aboard Dusty. The wolf took off on his stretched-out lope, occasionally looking back to ensure Sean was following, and within less than a hundred yards, he stopped and dropped on his haunches, awaiting the man and horses.

Sean stepped down, ground-tied the horses, and with Indy at his side, walked forward. Before him lay the wide trail of a buffalo herd. The ground had been trampled and churned by the passing herd of woolies, with the wide path looking like a dark swath painted across the moonlit prairie. Sean estimated the herd to be several hundred if not over a thousand. All cactus, grass, sage, and any living thing had been obliterated by the massive beasts. Sean and Indy walked across the swath, using the brightness of the moon to give aid as they searched for signs of hunters, both Indian and white men, but the only identifiable tracks were of the buffalo. Horses had not passed in pursuit of the herd.

As they walked back to the horses, Sean spoke to Indy, "Well, boy, where there's buffalo, there's soon to be natives on the hunt. This time o' year there won't be any big hunts, cuz the hides'll all be skimpy an' thin, not like in the fall or winter when they've got their cold weather coats on, but they're still good eatin'. So, if there's Indians around, you can bet they'll be huntin' up some fresh buffalo steaks."

Back on the move, he recognized the country where he and his pa had chased down the captors of Reindeer Fawn, the daughter of Jacques Bottineau and Red Leaf, of the Métis and Dakota who traveled with them when they guided the Buffalo Brigade. He rode the east side of Muskrat creek for several miles, and when it turned to the west, toward the hills, the low-lying clouds to the east had just begun to show a hint of red. It was time to call an end to the night's journey and find a well-hidden camp-site that offered graze and water as well as cover. He followed the Muskrat creek into the mouth of the canyon. The remaining moonlight dispelled the long shadows just enough to reveal a cutback into a west pointing draw. As he explored it, Sean saw it held a cluster of juniper and a trickle of spring water that was just enough to entice him to make his camp.

His feet had no more than touched the ground, when an early rising wolf, probably on a distant hilltop, said his sorrowful good-bye to the retreating darkness with a long, rising howl. Both Sean and Indy froze, looking and listening to the distant cry, wondering if it was a lone wolf, or the call to summon a hunting pack back to their lair. Barely heard from an even greater distance, rose the mournful cry that answered the first, and the prairie was silent as all the creatures that could appear on the wolf's menu, considered their own retreat.

Sean looked at Indy, saw the wolf, standing with one paw raised and ears perked, and spoke softly, "Anybody you know?"

Indy turned, relaxed his stance and trotted to Sean's side for some attention, and the man gladly rewarded both man and beast as he dropped to his knees and wrapped his arms around the wolf's neck and hugged him close. After a good rub behind his ears, Indy gave Sean a wet slobbery slurp with his tongue, and Sean leaned back on his heels, wiping his face with his sleeve. "I know you love me, but enough with the slobbers!"

Once free of their trappings, the horses took a frisky roll in the dirt and grass, stood patiently while Sean rubbed them down with handfuls of grass, and after a good long drink of the spring water, lazily began to graze on the green grasses at stream's edge. The thin line of grey marked the eastern horizon as Sean started his cookfire on the lee side of a sizable juniper, making certain the dim smoke from the dry wood would be dispersed by the branches of the juniper. But he planned on having the fire well out when full daylight painted the flats, for he was here to see and not to be seen. A quick breakfast of Johnny cakes and thin sliced pork belly and fresh hot coffee made a satisfying meal for the young traveler. When he covered over the coals to ensure there was no more smoke or smells, he stretched out on his bedroll between two piñon, and with Indy at his side, he was almost instantly asleep. It had been a long night, and he and the animals had traveled far; all deserved a good rest. When the sun crested the eastern horizon, the only sounds that came from the mouth of Muskrat Canyon was the soft cushioned steps of moccasins following the tracks and blood drops of a deer that staggered alongside the waters of Muskrat Creek.

CHAPTER SIX
RAWHIDE

WHEN THE TWO YOUNG WARRIORS RODE INTO THE VILLAGE shouting, those nearby gathered, anxious for a good report. Most knew several warriors had been dispatched to search for the migrating buffalo and they hoped these men brought news. It had been a long winter, and their stores of meat and dried vegetables had been almost exhausted, and hunger threatened the village of nearly fifty lodges. It was urgent they locate the spring migration for their first hunt. "Thatháŋka!" "Buffalo!" shouted the warriors, as they dropped to the ground to run toward the lodge of the village chief, Crow Dog.

As the stately man stepped through the hide flap of his tipi and tossed it aside, he stood and scowled at the messengers. The older of the two excitedly reported of their sighting of a large herd of buffalo east of the long ridge of mountains that lay south of their village. The Brulé camp was spread out on the flats between the snake-like rocky-topped ridge on the east and the flat-top buttes on the west, where the Silver Springs Creek watered the valley bottom and gave ample graze for their horse herd and water for the village. The buffalo were reported to be moving slowly northward near the alkali flats that lay to the east of the long finger ridges of juniper and piñon.

The chief looked at the gathering crowd and held his hands high, "It is good! We can make the hunt and not have to move our village. Let all the warriors prepare; we leave soon!" The crowd scattered, chattering like excited children, moving like scared rabbits, and all anxious and hopeful at the prospects of their first spring hunt. No more would there be empty pots and hungry bellies, the great *Wakan Tanka* has brought the buffalo!

In short order, the warriors that would go on the hunt were assembled near the lodge of Crow Dog. Their *Wicasa Wakan* or Holy Man stood before them and chanted a prayer to *Wakan Tanka* for a bountiful hunt, and as he lowered his arms, the crowd of hunters shouted and swung aboard their favorite buffalo ponies, kicking them to a run for their pursuit of the buffalo.

———

BY MID-DAY a restless Indy stirred Sean to wakefulness, and the grumpy sleepyhead groaned and grunted as he rolled from his blankets. In that instant, he knew he had made a mistake. His father always taught, "Whenever anything wakes you, never move anything but your eyes. Whatever it is that has caught your attention, may be close by and you may be in danger. Always look and listen before you move, and always have a weapon at hand." He was instantly awake and reached for his rifle laying on the scabbard beside the blanket, and with it in hand, he dropped to one knee, back against the low branches of the juniper. Indy was crouched under the tree, watching something in the creek bottom below. Sean realized he was holding his breath and let it slowly escape as he searched the willows and grasses along the creek bank.

Barely visible across the creek and in the willows, he saw movement and kept his eyes moving up and down the stream for any other sign of trouble. As he watched, he made out the figure of an Indian working on something on the ground. Sean looked back at his saddle and bags, retrieved the brass scope left to him by his father, and slowly extended it to full length to better watch the movement below. A young Indian, probably Sioux, was finishing dressing out a deer, undoubtedly taken at least an hour earlier. Sean looked down at Indy and whispered, "Some lookout you are! He coulda scalped us both an' you wouldn'ta done a thing!"

Tethered to a scraggly piñon behind the man was a black horse with three white stocking legs. The animal was contentedly grazing, occasionally looking up to see what his rider was doing. Sean watched until the man secured two hide bundles of meat, balanced on each side of his horse, then swung up behind them and with a broad smile on his satisfied face, trotted to the mouth of the canyon and disappeared around the protruding finger ridge.

Sean sat back on his rump, breathed a little easier, and thought out what he should do; either wait till dark to move, or follow the buffalo and the hunter to see if he could find the Sioux village without being spotted himself. He reached for the left-over Johnny Cakes and munched on the cold patties as he thought. He looked to Indy, "Boy, I think we'll see if we can locate that herd and keep a look-out to see if the Sioux mount a hunt. I'm thinkin' that'll save us a lotta wanderin' around tryin' to find 'em. We'll just let them come to us!"

Satisfied with his decision, he gathered up his gear and saddled up the horses. At the mouth of the canyon, Sean ground tied the horses, and climbed the shoulder of the hill that overlooked the wide valley beyond. The Rawhide Creek wound its way between the lower ridge of hills behind him and three timbered buttes to the east. The tracks of the lone deer hunter appeared to follow the creek in the bottom to the north, but the wide swath of the buffalo stayed on the far side of the buttes in the buffalo-grass flats. He searched the valley bottom, and as far as he could see both upstream and down, all he saw was the tiny figure of the lone hunter well upstream and moving away. Sean crabbed away from the crest and walked back to the horses, picked up the lead for the packhorse and the reins of Dusty and mounted up. He looked down at Indy, "We're goin' 'crost the valley, but we'll stay in the low draws and ravines until we get to those buttes beyond. Then we'll find us a good look-out high-up and watch for the Sioux to come after the buffalo. Understand? Now, don't go lettin' any more o' them fellas come sneakin' up on you!" With a wave of his hand, he sent Indy on the path before him.

Crossing of the valley of the Rawhide Creek took less than an hour, and he was soon following the tree-line of the buttes as he rode the up and down of the finger ridges and bluffs. He had spotted a dead-end draw that offered ample cover among the juniper for him to make a day camp and leave his horses. His objective was the highest of the three buttes that offered an excellent promontory and cover for him to glass the herd and any band of hunters that might pursue them. He was certain that if there was a village nearby, and the lone hunter would suggest that, they would soon mount a hunt for the buffalo.

Sean was pleased to find the draw was as he hoped. Two high timber-covered ridges boxed in the grassy bottomed draw that held a hat-sized seep of fresh water, all sheltered behind thick juniper. He loosened the cinches, tethered the horses, stuck the scope in his buckskin tunic, and with the Spencer in hand, he started the climb to the top of the biggest butte of the three. As he worked his way in a zig-zag fashion to the top, he found layers and wide strips of sedimentary rock that lay like a line of pillows across the top of the ridge. The hard lines of reddish-grey stone pointed the way to the summit of the big butte.

Sean stayed below the ridge, not wanting to skyline himself and moved slowly among the juniper and cedar, knowing that movement attracted attention. He cautiously picked his steps, and shortly came to the crest. He bellied down, moved to a wide, flat rock and pulled out the telescope. He shielded the end with his open palm, preventing any reflection that would give away his location and slowly scanned the wide flats below. The blue and purple of the basin was covered with a dark brown wool blanket of buffalo. The animals were contentedly grazing on the fresh spring grass, but they kept close to one another. As Sean watched, he saw a few of the cows calving, others with orange fur balls at their side taking their nourishment, while several herd bulls moseyed along the edge, watching for predators. This was the time that attracted wolves, cougars, coyotes, and even a few bears. The temptation of taking a vulnerable new-born calf, the smells of afterbirth and blood, and defenseless mothers giving birth, attracted every manner of predator.

Sean scanned the herd, and something caught his attention. He paused, and searched again, watching as the burly beasts ambled in the grasses. There it was again; he focused the glass on a group of cows, two with calves at their side, one turned away but apparently with a calf on the far side. He watched and waited, and as the mother took a few steps forward, the calf was revealed. All white! Apparently, it was one of the early calves, bigger than many of the others, but moving comfortably beside his mother. He was pushing at the back of his mother's belly, wanting to get his dinner.

Sean remembered what his pa had said, and what White Feather, the Comanche medicine woman and close friend of his family, had explained about the belief of almost all the plains Indians that a white buffalo was a sacred animal. The presence of one in a herd, gave the nearby tribes hope of blessings, bounty, and favor from the Creator. His friend, Fawn of the Dakota people, told him the Dakota and the Lakota people believed that *Wakan Tanka* or the Great Spirit taught that *Ptehin-calaskawin,* or White Buffalo Calf Woman, was the Holy Woman that led her people. Sean knew the white calf was important, but he had no idea what the Sioux would do when they saw him.

Indy was belly down beside him, and Sean looked at his friend, "Well, boy, this might change things considerable. Guess we'll just have to wait and see!"

CHAPTER SEVEN
PREDATORS

As Sean watched the grazing buffalo and searched for any sign of the Sioux, he moved from the peak of the butte to a timbered shoulder that offered better cover and at least a little shade from the afternoon sun. He had settled down on a rocky promontory where a gnarly cedar shielded him from view and stretched its branches across the rocks. He found a mossy patch in the shadow of a large boulder and bellied down for another scan. He turned the brass tube to the north and saw movement. A band of mounted warriors sat watching from a slight rise, showing only their shoulders and heads above the crest. One impressive figure with a single braid over one shoulder, feathers at the back of his head in a scalplock, a beaded band above his bicep, and a bone breast-plate on his chest, seemed to be barking orders to the others. As he pointed, several moved to either side and stationed themselves where directed.

Sean continually scanned with his scope and saw several hunters on foot, working their way down a dry gulch that cut across the flat. When he swung the scope back to the leader, he saw his raised hand drop and the knoll belched the hunters on horseback as they lunged toward the herd. Sean followed their pursuit, noting the mounted hunters were making a wide sweep toward him and the edge of the herd, apparently to try to move the animals toward the hunters in the gulch. Sean watched, amazed at the horsemanship of the riders, guiding the horses with their legs as they nocked arrows and leaned into their shots to send the feathered missiles into the thick fur of the buffalo. Several with lances moved their horses beside the wooly beasts, matching them step for step as they thrust flint-tipped spears into the ribs of their prey. One warrior pursued his target into the midst of the herd and Sean saw the Indian launched over the head of the falling horse as a big bull hooked his horn into the horse's side, ripping it open and the herd trampled horse and rider into the dirt.

Sean guessed there were forty or fifty hunters, most on horseback. It wasn't until the herd started stampeding toward the gulch that Sean heard gunshots. He realized that all the mounted hunters were using only bows and lances, and the men with rifles were the trap. Like a brown tidal wave, the herd swerved away from the onslaught of thunderous weapons, and Sean saw the leader, the man he thought was the chief, riding his horse at the side of the herd, but waving a blanket to the hunters, frantically trying to get them to stop. As the herd moved away from the gulch, many of the hunters climbed from the ravine and walked toward the waiting chief, now sitting his horse but waving the blanket overhead toward the mounted hunters.

As the warriors gathered by the chief, Sean moved his scope toward the saddle in the far hills and saw a line of people coming toward the hunting ground, women leading horses pulling travois, children, and others, walking and waving their arms toward the hunters. These were the wives and other women of the village, come to do their part in butchering the carcasses and hauling the meat back to the people. It was going to be a long afternoon of hard work of skinning and parting out the kills. Sean moved the glass back over the killing grounds and was surprised there weren't more carcasses. He counted at most maybe eighteen downed buffalo. With that many hunters, but most armed with bows and lances, he expected to see at least one per hunter. But the chief had called off the hunt before the ambush was successful. Sean nodded his head as he spoke softly to Indy, "Musta finally seen the white calf and called 'em off. Now what?"

It appeared as organized chaos when the many villagers swarmed onto the killing ground to take care of the downed buffalo. Several warriors gathered around the carcass nearest their group and were soon passing the blood-dripping liver around for each hunter to have a chunk. Some sliced off their portion, dipping it into the bile and munching on the bloody meat, while others simply took the end in their mouth, and with a deft move with their knives, cut off the portion held in their teeth and handed the remaining piece to the next man.

Excitement ran high both for the successful hunt and for the sighting of the white buffalo calf, with warriors and women alike dancing around, waving their arms and shouting at one another. It was common for a great feast and dance to follow the hunt, often taking place on the hunting ground. Sean saw a small group gathered around the leader, all seated on the ground, and animatedly talking about what Sean assumed would be the tale of the hunt and the calf. While each carcass was stripped, cut up, and portions piled on the fresh hides on the travois, the women moved from one buffalo to another.

Sean was reminded of his mother's saying that "Many hands make light work!" As he watched the activity, he saw movement at the edge of the scene of the killing. He saw several coyotes, two wolves, a bobcat, too many ravens to count, dozens of turkey buzzards, several hawks, and even a pair of eagles. At each gut and bone pile, fights between the carrion eaters were constant, each fighting for their portion. It was the banquet of the plains, and no one wanted to miss out. Animals that would never be seen in close proximity in the wild, now ravenously dined side by side.

It was nearing dusk when the activity and numbers dwindled. Small groups, each with at least one horse and travois, often more, had started in the direction of the village. As Sean watched, he saw some of the warriors leading their war-horses loaded with bundles of meat wrapped in hides, and walking side-by-side with their women and children. The killing grounds had been left to the predators of the prairie and Sean knew some of the big boys, like cougars and maybe black bears, would soon join the banquet, chasing the lesser ones from the better piles.

He lifted his scope, looking at the herd that had moved both north and east away from the presence of death. The distance of separation was no more than a mile or maybe a little more, but the wooly giants of the prairie grazed as if it was just another day on the plains. And of course, that was exactly what it was, for these animals had few predators other than man and fear was not often realized by creatures that often weighed a ton or more. As he scanned the herd looking for the white calf, he saw one young bull at the edge of the herd, limping as he sought to stay near the rest. Probably wounded by an arrow, this bull would eventually fall to those predators that preyed on the weak and sickly or young and helpless.

Sean looked down to Indy, "Maybe that's my chance to get some fresh buffalo steak!" He shimmied back from his point on the rocks, and with the wolf at his side, he quickly made his way back to the tethered horses. He knew he would need a travois to handle all that meat, too much for one packhorse, and there were no trees in the flats. But in the valley below, there were a couple patches of cottonwood that might yield a pair of saplings that would serve his purpose. He made short work of fashioning the saplings, lashed them to the side of the pack to drag behind the dapple-grey and they were soon on their way to the herd.

He staked the horses in a dry gulch, out of sight of the herd, then with longbow and quiver in hand, he began his stalk. It was easy work in the dim twilight, and he was soon near enough to the limping bull to take his shot. He slowly stood, stepped into his bow bringing the arrow to full draw and quickly loosed it to the target. The bull lunged forward, took a half-dozen staggering steps, and fell to the side, with little disturbance to the nearby animals.

The moon was high and the stars bright when Sean finished his work. The boned meat and larger bones were stacked and lashed on the travois, and the dapple-grey leaned into his work. Sean had lightened the panniers as best he could by putting some of the weight on the travois or behind the cantle of his saddle, but it was a task for the horses to haul their usual gear, Sean, and the additional weight of a buffalo.

While he was working on the carcass, Sean and Indy heard the lonesome wail of a wolf or two, and Sean thought little of it. But when he was ready to go, Indy was nowhere to be seen. Sean shook his head but wasn't worried; he had seen both Lobo and Indy take off on their own looking for their own prey or even company. Indy was a mature male, and in the wilderness would probably be a leader of his own pack, so it wasn't a matter of concern for the black wolf to take a foray into the night of his own accord. Sean knew Indy would probably be at his side by the time he rolled from his blankets come morning. He had decided to make camp for the night and scout out the village either in the early morning or wait until nightfall tomorrow. Now he was tired and anxious to get reacquainted with his bedroll.

WHEN INDY LAY beside the carcass and chewed on a meat-covered bone, trying to crack it to get to the marrow, he perked up at the sound of a distant cry of a wolf. This was not the wail of a lonesome female looking for a partner, or even the challenge of a male. This was the call of a pack-leader for his pack to come. Indy looked at Sean and the horses, back in the direction of the call and when it came again, he stood, ears perked, and took a tentative step forward. With another look over his shoulder at the busy man at the gut pile, he trotted off into the darkness.

When Indy neared the trees at the base of the butte, he saw a flicker of firelight and smelled man, horse, and blood. With another deep sniff, he also recognized the smell of afterbirth. It had been a short while since he heard the wolf howl, but he also caught the smell of wolves in the midst of the bitterness of the cedar and piñon. Indy lowered his head, cautiously trotting toward the smells of man and blood, knowing the wolf pack was coming from higher up and probably going to the same scent.

Before he cleared the trees, he heard a shout! He knew there would be someone by the fire, and he kept his pace in that direction. When he came to the edge of the clearing, he saw four wolves, the pack leader, his mate, and two others. They were spread out, the leader at the point and the mate slightly behind, all with heads down, mouths snarling, eyes squinting, and the leader letting the rumble of a growl fill the clearing. On the far side stood a paint horse, obviously a mare, that had just dropped a foal that lay with legs entangled, covered with afterbirth, and the mare licking at the placenta. Between the small fire and the mare, an Indian woman held a knife in one hand and a flaming brand in the other. She stepped forward, shouted and waved the torch, but the wolves never wavered in their stalk. Two started to one side, two to the other, nearing the woman and readying to attack.

The pack leader took one slow step, another, the points of his shoulders pushing up at the base of his neck looking like deformed humps of grey, his body slowly lowered as he prepared to lunge for the woman. His hind legs tensed and pushed. He lifted from the ground, mouth wide, fangs dripping, a growl roared from his throat, and he stretched out his forepaws, when suddenly a streak of black came from the side and knocked the wolf to the ground. The midnight fur with hackles raised, buried its teeth into the throat of the pack leader and shook his head back and forth, snapping the neck-bones as the other three were frozen in their stances. Each of the remaining wolves watched as their leader kicked and squirmed helplessly in the death grip of his attacker. Then the mate started to attack, but the big black wolf, teeth still buried in the throat of the leader, swung the entire carcass in front of the mate, stopping her charge.

Between the woman and the mate stood Indy, in his killing stance, teeth bared and dripping the blood of his kill, orange eyes flashing in the firelight, and a threatening growl coming from deep in his belly as he faced the threatening pack. The mate cowered, tucked her tail, hunched her back, and dropped her head, looking at the intruder from the corner of her eyes. The other two saw the she-wolf cower, but the larger of the two lowered his head and threatened the interloper with a growl and bared fangs. Indy turned his attention to the new threat, and before the grey could attack, Indy lunged at him, bowling him over and turned to grab the grey's neck in his jaws. He held the animal still, growling, threatening, watching the other two tuck tails and whimper as they started to move away. Indy clamped tighter, and with a sudden jerk to the side, snapped the grey wolf's neck and dropped the lifeless form at his feet.

Indy stood, head up, looking at the two dead wolves, then back to the woman. He opened his mouth, tongue lolling and wagged his tail. With one more look at the dead wolves, another at the woman, Indy trotted off into the woods in search of his friend and family, Sean and the horses. He left behind an astounded woman, watching him leave, standing immobile for several minutes expecting the wolf to return, but when he didn't, she dropped to her knees, sat back on her haunches and stared at the fire. The words she whispered were in the white man's tongue, words she hadn't used in a long time. "No one will believe me, no one."

CHAPTER EIGHT
VILLAGE

As Sean expected, Indy was lying beside him when he awoke at the first light of morning. He listened, hearing nothing but the occasional stomp of his horses and the early song of a meadowlark. He looked from side to side before moving his head and saw the flicker of gray as a whiskey jack prowled the camp for tidbits. With nothing alarming the birds, wolf, or horses, Sean thought it safe to roll from his blankets. Before turning in last night, he had pushed north a couple miles and found a suitable camp in a side draw off a saddle crossing of the long ridge with sparse timber. The cluster of juniper surrounded a small basin that held a pool of run-off water that suited the horses, but wasn't too appealing to him.

He scratched around to find enough dry wood for a hat-sized fire to brew some coffee. He filled the pot from his canteen and with a triangle of rocks, sat the pot over the small flames. He fed the fire with sticks no bigger than his fingers, always watching the whisper of smoke to ensure it was dispersed by the overhanging branches. He was a little uncomfortable having a fire in the morning, but his appetite wasn't satisfied with the two left-over Johnny cakes and the handful of pemmican. Once the coffee brewed, he doused the fire with dirt, sat back and poured a cup of the tantalizing brew, savoring the smell as much as the flavor.

With his cravings sated, he climbed the slope for a look around. For a land that was abuzz with activity the day before, there was nothing moving this morning. The buffalo had moved farther to the northeast, grazing on the spring green flats and moving toward the Niobrara River. Directly north of his position, about five miles distant, was where he thought he would find the camp of the Sioux. It was a green valley, well protected between some flat-top buttes and a long line of intermittent hills that lay south of the Niobrara. Beyond that, it was another fifteen to twenty miles to good cover and ample water and grass for the horses.

With a thorough survey of the country round about, Sean spent his usual morning time greeting the day with a few moments in prayer. He walked back to the trees and sat down, poured the last of the warm coffee into his tin cup, sat, sipped, and thought. He remembered the times he and his pa had visited other Indian camps, some where he was known, and others where he was a stranger, but welcomed. "Son, most native people have respect for courage and honesty. And, most have a practice that while you're in their village, nothing bad will happen to you, it's kind of a hospitality thing. The trouble is, there's no way of knowing which village will be friendly and which one will try to take your hair as soon as you show your face. So, it's a bit risky, but I usually prefer to just ride or walk right in as if you owned the place. Show yourself friendly, and they'll usually accept you as such."

Sean considered his father's sage advice, shook his head and mumbled, "Yeah, but you ain't here pa, and it's my hair they'll be lookin' at!" Indy had lifted his head at the man's words, lay his chin on Sean's leg and lifted his sorrowful eyes to him. Sean chuckled, rubbed Indy's scruff, "Yeah, a lot you know. You run off after some howling, she-wolf and leave me to fend for myself!"

He looked at the hide-covered bundles of buffalo meat, looked up at the cloudless sky and thought he would either have to stay in camp to smoke and dry the meat, or haul it to the village and let some lonesome old widow woman have at it. He looked back down at Indy, rubbed behind his ears, "Let's go, boy. If I'm gonna get scalped, no sense puttin' it off till tomorrow!"

WHEN SEAN RODE from behind the round top hill, he looked at the limestone lines that appeared as concentric circles climbing the hillside. He thought it might have been underwater at some time and that the lines were the water level marks as the lake receded. But across the valley, the flat top buttes on the east side had no such marks. He looked to the village, guessing the number of lodges somewhere around fifty; a sizeable village. All the entries faced east, and he approached slightly south of due east. He was about a hundred fifty yards from the nearest tipi when the alarm sounded that someone had seen him. He looked down at Indy, walking close beside Dusty and slightly ahead, "Easy boy, stay close now," he warned. He drew a deep breath, squared his shoulders to sit high in his saddle and with his left hand loosely holding the reins, right hand at his side, he used his body weight and leg pressure to keep Dusty moving.

Three warriors had swung aboard their horses and with lances waving, ran toward the approaching white man. They shouted, and taunted, trying to frighten him, but Sean kept his eyes forward, looking to the passageway between the lodges that led to the central compound. He didn't hesitate or respond to their taunts. One warrior struck him on the shoulder with a coup stick, but Sean kept his eyes forward and kept Dusty moving. When one of the warrior's horses came too near, Indy lowered his head and growled, frightening the horse, causing it to start bucking and fleeing. The rider grabbed a handful of mane, tried to pull his mount back, and when the horse dropped his head between his forelegs and tried to kick a hole in the blue sky, the warrior lost his grip and somersaulted over the animal's withers, landing on his back and losing his wind. He lay gasping for air as several youngsters pointed and laughed.

With their attention focused on the man, the others had not seen Indy, but now they shied back away from this white man and the big wolf that trotted beside him, hackles raised and fangs showing. Sean did his best to keep from chuckling and maintain a somber expression, but the corners of his mouth tugged, and he let a slow smile show. When the villagers saw that expression, they grinned and began to follow the white man that showed no threat. Sean did notice several warriors following, each with arrows nocked but held down at their side. One man had a rifle cradled in his arms and he walked near. He lifted his hand and asked in the Lakota tongue, "Why are you here?"

The speaker was surprised when Sean answered in the same tongue, "I bring meat for your old women. There is too much for me. This buffalo was wounded when your warriors hunted, I took him and now bring the meat to your people."

"You speak our language well. Where did you learn this?" The man continued walking beside Sean, on the opposite side of Indy, keeping his eye on the wolf.

"I have friends among the Dakota, those of the Santee."

"What are you called?"

"I am Bear Chaser." At the name that was unusual for a white man, the speaker looked up at Sean, showing surprise. "I wish to speak with your chief, visit with your people."

They had come to the central compound, and the people spread out around the wide clearing. A fire pit with smoldering coals was in the center, a woman tending a pot of food who looked at Sean as if he was no different than any others nearby. The horses stopped, the speaker motioned for Sean to dismount and held Dusty's reins to subtly control the animal. Sean motioned to Indy to sit, then he stood to the side of Dusty as the flap of the larger tipi was flipped aside, and a stern-faced warrior emerged. Sean recognized him as the leader of the hunters and knew he must be the chief of the village.

The chief walked up to Sean, looked at him then turned his attention to the horses and the travois of meat, but when he saw the big wolf, his eyes grew large in surprise and he looked back at Sean. Suddenly a young woman stepped beside the chief, "Father, that is the black wolf! That's the one that killed the others! I told you! See!" Her excited exclamations and gestures startled the chief and he turned to scowl at the anxious woman, silencing her with his look. She dropped her head and stepped back, mumbling, "I am sorry, father."

Sean had understood everything the woman said, and he leaned around Dusty to look at Indy, "So that's where you were last night!" Indy just grinned, open-mouthed, tongue lolling, and looked from Sean to the woman.

The man that followed beside him stepped forward, "My chief, this man is called Bear Chaser, he has brought meat for the old women."

The chief listened, looking at Sean, and asked, "You speak our tongue?"

"Yes," Sean answered simply.

The first speaker said, "He took a wounded buffalo after the hunt and brings the meat to our people."

"This is true, Bear Chaser?"

"Yes."

The chief looked from Sean to the warrior, and back to Sean, "I am Crow Dog, this man is called Afraid of His Horses." He looked to Sean again, "My daughter came today and told a story that we could not believe, but now she says this is the wolf she saw. Is it possible?"

"Yes, but what was the story?" asked Sean, forcing himself to maintain a somber expression.

Crow Dog turned to bring the woman forward, "This is White Fox." He motioned for her to speak, and she timidly began, often looking down to Indy as she spoke. This was the first time many of the people had heard the story of what had happened the night before, and there was a chattering among them as they listened. She concluded with, "He stood before me like a warrior to protect me. The two wolves were dead at his feet, and the others slinked off. He," motioning toward Indy, "turned back to look at me, and it was like he smiled at me, then trotted off into the trees." She looked to Sean to see if he believed her.

Sean slowly smiled, then snapped his fingers and motioned for Indy to come to his side. Several people drew back, speaking in whispers to one another as they watched the big wolf trot to the side of the white man. With a simple motion, Sean directed Indy to sit by his side. He looked down, "Indy, this is White Fox. Is she your friend?" The wolf rose and slowly stepped toward the woman, ran his nose from her knee to her waist, opened his mouth as he sat on his haunches and looked up at the woman, tongue lolling to the side. She slowly stretched out her hand to touch the side of the wolf's face, then reached farther to the scruff of his neck and as Indy leaned into her touch. She smiled and ran her fingers through his fur.

The chief looked at the wolf, then to Sean, "You will stay with us for a time?"

"If that's alright with you, chief. I would like to visit with your people so we can know each other better."

The chief motioned to a woman, standing alone, with a touch of grey in her hair, and she came forward. "This is Spotted Antelope, she will cook for you, and you will stay in her lodge. If you choose to share the meat, she will do that. We will speak tomorrow." Crow Dog turned back to his lodge, entered and dropped the flap, leaving Sean with Spotted Antelope, Afraid of His Horses, and White Fox. When the old woman motioned for him to follow, Sean reached for Dusty's reins, but Afraid of His Horses turned away and led the horses to follow the woman. White Fox stepped beside Sean and spoke, "I will go with you and the black wolf."

"His name is Indy. It's short for Indigo which means black," responded Sean as they followed the horses.

"It is strange that you have a wolf as a companion."

Sean chuckled, "My family has always had animals. When I was younger, we had a grey wolf and a cinnamon bear. They were called Lobo and Buster."

Fox turned to look at the man, trying to determine if he was speaking the truth, and was pleased to see that he was quite serious. "Will you stay with us long?"

"Oh, I don't know. I would like to learn more about your people."

"I will teach you. But I am not Brulé, I was taken by the Comanche when I was young, and the Brulé captured me from the Comanche. But I have been with Crow Dog and his woman for many years, and they are my family now."

Sean paused in his steps and looked at the woman, "You're not white, are you?"

"No, I was from Sante Fe, and my father was a trader. He was killed by the Comanche when I was taken as a small child. I have a few memories, but I can speak the language of my father and of the many white traders."

They resumed their walk and were at the cookfire by the entry of the old woman's lodge. Fox explained, "Spotted Antelope lost her man this past winter, and she had no children. What you have done has brought honor to her. She will care for you like a son." Sean looked from the old woman to White Fox as she said, "I will see you tomorrow to tell you about our people."

CHAPTER NINE
BRULÉ

SHE FOUND HIM HIGH UP ON THE EASTERN SLOPE OF THE flat-top butte west of the village. He had retreated for his morning prayer and sat watching the beginning of the day. The underbellies of dark clouds caught the muted pink of the yet-to-rise sun that offered the only color to the shadowy morning. The old woman told White Fox where the white man known as Bear Chaser had gone and she, with her natural stealth, climbed after him. She paused behind a twisted cedar, watching the man with his face lifted, eyes closed, arms spread wide, with his lips moving but no words that came to her hearing. She too was a person of prayer, and her worship was given to *Wakan Tanka* or the Great Spirit, and as she watched, she wondered if there was any difference between them and their gods.

A stone rolled under her foot, and she caught herself, letting a slight gasp escape, and she looked to the white man who watched her as she neared. "I do not mean to disturb you," she said as she seated herself on the edge of the same slab of rock.

"You didn't. I heard you coming for some time," answered Sean. "I'm glad you came." He turned to look at the colors in the east, nodded that direction, "It looks like it's going to be a stormy day, but the rain will be good. It's been a dry spring."

"This is true." She looked to the east, the colors now showing brighter and with a hint of orange added to the reddish pinks. In the moments of silence, they sat unmoving, watching the Creator paint the skies and the clouds, announcing the coming of day.

Sean looked at the woman, guessed her to be about his age, and enjoyed her beauty. Her long, straight hair caught the colors and showed a hint of glow, but the raven's wing black shone its own beauty. Her high cheekbones accented the depth of her dark eyes that reflected the colors of the eastern sky. The shape of her nose contrasted with the usual aquiline look of those of her tribe, it was finely shaped, perfectly sloped and a slight upturn to the petite form. Her lips were pouty, but in a smile that ended in dimpled cheeks. Her chin had a slight cleft, the neck was long, and the oval shape of her face was framed by her smooth long hair. She was taller than most women of the village, but still had to look up to Sean. Her trim figure was accented by the fitted tunic that held a crest of bead-work across the shoulders. Her leggings were fringed, and she brought one knee up and clasped her hands around it as she leaned back, smiling, soaking up the warmth of the sun that now peeked over the horizon. Sean believed she was what anyone would call beautiful.

. . .

THEY CLIMBED to the top of the butte, finding a break in the rimrock that offered a route to the flat-top. As they climbed, they talked. Each asking questions of the other, learning about their different lives and peoples. When they reached the top, they walked to the east edge, sat with feet dangling over the rimrock and looked at the valley below and the plains beyond.

"Our people, the Lakota, came from there," she pointed to the east and north. "We were part of the Dakota people, but our band moved to the west and became the Lakota. There are several bands, the Brulé, the Oglala, the Miniconjou, the Hunkpapa, and others. Our language is the same but different with each band." She dropped her head, searching her thoughts, and looked to Sean. "My father, Crow Dog, has said our people have always fought for our land, our way of life, our people. When we were driven from the land in the far east," she looked to the east as if seeing the land of the Dakota hundreds of miles away, "we had to fight other tribes for this land. And when the soldiers and others, Bridger, Fremont, and more, made the treaty of Horse Creek, what your people call the treaty of Fort Laramie, the treaty that was to give us what we already had, our territory, they called it. We still have to fight. They said our territory was from the Missouri River where the sun rises, to the Heart River in the north," she nodded to the east and pointed to the north, "to the Powder River where the sun sets, and to the North Platte." She nodded to the south where the North Platte carved its way. "But they said some of our land was to be for the Crow, the Assiniboine, and the Arikara. We had to fight to take our land back from these enemies of our people. The treaty also said we should let the whites pass through our land, they would go to a far land, away from here, but that is not true. And yet they come, the long lines of white wagons with those that want our land. The treaty said they would not stay, but many do, and others search for gold and ruin our land and kill our people. The white man's paper said they would give us what we need to live, meat, guns and the powder and lead for them, other things, all we would need. But they do not."

They stood and walked across the flat-top, talking as they strolled. "When our people waited, hungry, for the payment from the soldiers, one cow wandered into the camp, and our hungry people killed it for meat. But your soldiers came, and when our chief, Conquering Bear, offered to pay for the cow, your soldiers killed him. When our men fought back and killed the soldiers, they said we were wrong. Then when the soldier general, the Butcher, came with all his soldiers, they killed almost a hundred of our people, many of them women and children, and took almost that many as prisoners, also mostly women and children.

"There have been times of peace, but we still must fight. The settlers' wagons still come, and the payment from the white man's leaders does not. If we are to live, we must fight. They say it is our territory, but they still come to take it."

As Sean walked, he listened, often shaking his head in wonder. Wonder as to the obstinacy of the government, and soldiers, and agents, wonder as to the blatant disregard of the white man for the native people. He looked to White Fox, "I know there have been many times when your people have been wronged, but not all white men are like that. Just like there are those among your people that do wrong, so too among my people." He paused, and asked, "Wasn't there a white man that was an agent for your people?"

"Yes, he is now with the Oglala. Thomas Twiss took a wife among the Oglala, and now lives with them. He is accepted as one of them. They say he is no longer a white man."

"There are those among the soldiers that say he stole from the goods that were to be given to the Sioux. That he took many of the supplies and sold them to other white men and kept the money. Did your people know of this?"

"Yes. There were things in the wagons that our people did not want and could not use. He took those things and sold them to help his own family."

"Is that what he said?"

"Yes."

Sean looked at Fox and decided to keep his silence for now. He thought it would do no good to tell her that the agent had been thought to take powder and lead and staples like sugar, salt, and other items that would easily be sold to traders. Items that her people needed, but did not receive, yet blamed the soldiers and white men for the failure to deliver their supplies or annuities. He thought the telling of it would only alienate these people from him and other whites for they believed in the agent Twiss, even though he had been removed from that post by Lincoln, because of the perceived thievery.

Sean decided to turn the conversation to more pleasant topics and asked, "Tell me about how you came to the Brulé? How you came to be a daughter of Crow Dog and his woman."

White Fox smiled and looked to Sean as she began, "I think I was maybe six summers old when the Sioux stole me from the Comanche. When I was brought to the village, Runs in Water, Crow Dog's woman, took me into her lodge and helped me to learn the way of the people. After one summer they had the fifth rite, or Hunkapi. The rite was performed by the Shaman, Little Goat, and the rite bonds those of the lodge as a family and together with *Wakan Tanka*. After that I was known as the daughter of Crow Dog and Runs in Water was my mother."

They sat down, again dangling their legs from the rimrock, and Sean asked, "Do you remember the Comanche language?" but he asked it in the language of the Comanche. Fox was surprised to hear him speak the language and looked at him for a moment before answering in the language of the Comanche. "Some, but it has been a long time."

"And you said you remember the language of your home, Sante Fe. But do you know any English?"

They were speaking in the language of the Lakota, but Fox answered in English. "Yes, I have learned the language since I was a young child. My father was white, but my mother was Mexican, and we spoke English. I have used the white man language when we go to the fort to trade."

Sean stood, helped Fox to her feet, "I have enjoyed this time, Fox. May we visit more?"

"If you stay with our village, we will visit and learn from each other," she smiled as she answered, dropping her eyes but looking back up, coyly.

"I would like that, but for now, I think Spotted Antelope might be looking for us. I was to help her divide up the meat today."

"I can help with that. It is woman's work anyway."

FOR THE NEXT THREE DAYS, Fox and Sean spent most of their time together. They were often seen walking with the big black wolf at their side, as they roamed through the village and into the nearby hills. They became very comfortable with one another, and both looked forward to their time together, until the day when a party of warriors returned to the village bearing lances with fresh scalps, obviously white scalps.

CHAPTER TEN
INDEPENDENCE

JAMES HARRIS AND THOMAS LAFFERTY WERE PARTNERS IN the First National Bank of Independence, the oldest and best capitalized bank in Independence, Missouri. Much of their fortune had been made supplying the fur trade, both with goods and capital that made it possible to ship furs and pelts from the mountains to Saint Louis. Now their attention had turned to the burgeoning frontier and the need for land for settlers. Many of the leaders of industry in the east believed the country was becoming too over-crowded and they must push further west to expand the nation. Although the partnership of Harris and Lafferty was well known and respected, they were also known for their ruthlessness in business dealings.

The man seated opposite them had come unexpected and unbidden, and they were a little apprehensive after he introduced himself as the new Commissioner of Indian Affairs, William P. Dole. His associate, a sizeable man with ill-fitting clothes for his large frame, stood beside the door, hands clasped at his waist, and unmoving. Dole began, "You gentlemen have some very influential friends in the capital. It was suggested that I make this visit as I begin my duties as commissioner. I understand you gentlemen own the warehouse where most of the goods are stored that are marked as annuities for the Indians, is that right?"

The partners were both dressed in frock coats with waistcoats, starched shirts, and cravats, with high waisted cotton trousers that were the fashion of the day. Harris sat behind the desk while Lafferty had one hip on the edge of the desk and one foot on the floor. Harris puffed on a cigar as he eyed the visitor through a haze of smoke. Lafferty answered for the partnership, "That is correct sir, the warehouse is one of a number of properties we hold."

"And is it not true that your quartermaster, as you call him, is responsible for the shipping of those goods to the west?"

"That is also correct. We have a contract with the government to supply the allotments for the different tribes. But what may I ask is the purpose of this questioning?"

Dole grinned, stood, and walked behind his chair as he took a thin cigar from an inside pocket, trimmed it, and leaned forward to use a long lucifer, holding the flame to the end of the cigar until it was properly lit, then put it in his lips, drew deeply and exhaled the smoke. He used the moment as a measure of control, keeping the partners waiting in suspense. He knew they knew he had the authority to cancel what was probably a very lucrative contract, and with the rumors of their less than honest dealings with the Indian agents, they could also be on the brink of legal trouble. He grinned as he sat down, crossed his legs, and looked from Lafferty to Harris and back to the speaker for the pair.

"When I accepted this appointment, I must admit I was somewhat disappointed. I had expected a commission in the Union Army. But, once I investigated this position and the many possibilities, I decided this could be very profitable and beneficial for me and anyone that was in agreement." He looked from one to the other of the men to gauge their attention and interest.

"Continue, please," said Harris as he leaned forward to rest his forearms on the desk.

"First, you need to understand, that I have done my due diligence in investigating everything having to do with this office. We have received complaints from different tribes through several agents and even through army posts. Those complaints have two things in common; one, that they do not receive all they were promised, and two, what they do receive is either spoiled or of no particular use to them." As he paused, he looked at the men, and Lafferty stood and started to object, but was stopped by Dole's uplifted hand.

"That is not the primary reason for my investigation. Personally, I think it is asinine to even consider providing the Indian with rifles and ammunition so they can murder innocent settlers! There is a lot of talk in Washington about reservations. That plan has worked very well for many different tribes that have been moved to Indian Territory, and I don't see why it cannot work for those tribes that seem to be so needy of these very valuable goods." He paused as he took another long draw on his cigar, uncrossed his legs, and leaned forward.

"Are either of you familiar with the Homestead Act?"

The partners looked to one another, then Lafferty replied, "Yes, that was the bill that wanted to offer free land to any settler that would take it, 160 acres I believe. But wasn't it vetoed by Buchanan?"

"After considerable pressure from the southern states, yes it was. But now with the war and the new president, I have it on good authority it will be signed into law."

"But I don't understand what that has to do with us?" commented Harris.

"Where do you think those settlers will find their homesteads?" asked Dole, cocking one eyebrow high in a question.

The partners looked at one another and at their visitor and as the realization of the opportunity before them, both slowly grinned. Lafferty leaned forward, "So, you believe the settlers will want the land now in Indian Territory?"

Dole smiled and nodded his head, "And with the war requiring the soldiers from the forts in the west that would control the Indians, like the troops from Fort Laramie that have been recalled to Jefferson Barracks in St. Louis, there will be little control over what happens out there. When the tribes get upset for not getting their annuities, and the settlers have no lands to homestead and the army busy with the war in the east, what do you suppose will be the outcome?"

"Well, that sounds like the makings of and Indian war, but how will that benefit us?" asked Harris, the partner that was always concerned about the details of any deal.

"If history is any proof, the Indians will eventually be put on reservations, and millions of acres will be available, first come, first served! And the more of your people that file homesteads, adjoining properties of course, the greater your holdings," declared Dole. "And, in the meantime, I'm certain enterprising gentlemen such as yourselves can see the opportunity in excess goods that happen to be stored in warehouses and don't make it to the turbulent areas of marauding Indians, am I right?"

As the afternoon meeting wore on, the three men hashed out the details of what they anticipated to be a very lucrative business venture. Details such as distribution of enough annuities to avoid questions from Washington, not that any were expected, considering all the turmoil with the war. The partners explained they also had holdings in Sante Fe and business connections there that gladly accepted any goods to be sold or traded for profit. Dole was willing to share his knowledge about the different agents that were cooperative with any endeavor that was profitable for them. But when the name of Thomas Twiss was mentioned, Dole questioned the men.

"He's the one that sent so many inquiries to the Commission, and he also has family connections in Washington. From what I understand, he was an honor graduate of West Point. Did you have dealings with him?" asked the Commissioner.

"Yes, and as long as he got his share, he was easy to deal with. But now that he has an Indian wife, and since Lincoln removed him as an agent, he might try to cause problems."

"Well, gentlemen, I guess you'll just have to give your distributor leeway to deal with the man. And I suppose, since he also has a wife in New York, perhaps he could be more easily persuaded to see things our way."

As they concluded their discussion, Dole stood,

extended his hand to shake with each of the partners, and said, "I will tend to things in Washington, you gentlemen can handle everything to the west, I'm sure." He nodded his head, deposited his card on the desk, and turned to leave. His companion opened the door for them, and the two men left the office. As they entered the carriage, the quiet companion stated, "You did not tell them of your percentage."

"No, Hubert, I did not. But it is of no interest to them. When Congress appropriates the amounts for the different tribes, it is my responsibility to procure the supplies and see they are sent. It is only natural and assumed that there will be considerable 'handling charges.' And I have complete freedom to assess the handling or shipping charge I deem to be appropriate."

CHAPTER ELEVEN
CONFRONTATION

THE RETURN OF THE WARRIORS CAUSED CONSIDERABLE excitement and celebration among the villagers. When their men gain honors with victories over their enemies, it is a shared honor among family and the rest of the band. A feast was prepared, and everyone joined in the work. Spotted Antelope drew Sean aside as soon as he and White Fox returned from their walk on the mountain.

"It is not good for you to be here. The warriors are showing their scalps and trophies and telling their stories." She looked from Sean to Fox, "And Blue Eagle has returned." Fox dropped her head as the old woman turned to Sean, "Blue Eagle has wanted to take Fox as his woman, but she did not want him. Her father has given her the freedom to make her own choice, but that is not usual for our people. If Blue Eagle knows of you, he will want to add your scalp to his lance."

"Well, that ain't too friendly of him!" declared Sean,

showing no concern. He looked to Fox, "Do you want me to go?"

"No, I have enjoyed our time together. I do not want it to end, but I do not want you to have to fight Blue Eagle. He is a great warrior and has taken many coup and scalps."

"If you do not want me to go, I will stay. Blue Eagle is not my enemy, but if he wants to fight, then we will fight."

"But, even if you were to take him, there are others. You are a white man, and their blood is hot to drive the white man from our lands. Our men live to fight. They have driven the Crow and the Arikara and the Assiniboine from our lands; now they want to drive the white man away. You cannot fight the whole village."

Spotted Antelope said, "I have brought your horses. They are behind the lodge. It is best if you wait for the feast and dance and when the sun is gone. They will not know of you until after you have gone."

Sean sat silent, lifted his eyes to White Fox, "If I go, I will come back. You have become very special to me."

Fox smiled, dropped her eyes, and stood to leave. She whispered something to the old woman and left the lodge. Spotted Antelope insisted he stay in the lodge while she prepared him a meal, and he used the time to gather his gear, clean his rifles, and load the panniers. Dusk had dropped its curtain when Antelope stepped into the lodge, a plate and cup in her hands, and motioned for Sean to be seated as she handed the offering to him. She sat beside him and spoke, "I have enjoyed having you in my lodge these few days. I lost my son two summers ago when he went on a raid against some white men that had rifles that shoot many times. It was beyond where the buffalo were."

Sean paused in his eating, remembering when he and his father had scouted for the buffalo brigade and had been in that same place at that time. It was a Brulé band that attacked them and took his friend, Fawn, as their captive. They had been forced to defend themselves against the attack, and most of the Indians had been killed. He dropped his eyes to his plate as she continued, "My husband also died, but he was fighting the Crow."

"You have been kind to take me into your lodge. You are a good woman."

"With you here, it is like having a son again."

Sean handed the woman his empty plate and cup, stood and started for the entry. He moved the flap aside enough to peer out, and satisfied there was no one near, turned back for his gear. Within moments, his horses were ready, and he said his goodbye to the woman, looked for Fox and not seeing her, mounted up. With one last look around, he put his heels to Dusty's ribs and started to leave.

"Ho! White man! Do you leave like the coward you are? Tuck your tail and run away like a cowering coyote!?" shouted Blue Eagle who stood beyond the lodge of Spotted Antelope, lance in hand, feet wide apart as he waved his arm overhead.

Sean twisted around in his saddle, saw the man and others coming behind him and answered, "I am Bear Chaser. I do not run! Are you the Blue bird I heard that sings his threats, puffs his chest to show his color, and pecks at the seeds others leave behind?!" Sean swung his leg over the pommel and slid to the ground to stand facing the loud threat.

Blue Eagle strode forward, waved his lance that held several scalps, as if the sight would intimidate the white man. He shouted again, "I will add your scalp to my lance!" He tossed it up just enough to change his grip, readying to throw it, stepped forward and cocked his arm back.

Sean watched, knowing what the man threatened, and as he leaned back to launch his lance, Sean drew and cocked the Colt, lifted it and fired, the bullet breaking the lance just behind the head, and startling the warrior.

"Aiieee! You are like the rest of the cowardly white men! You must use your weapons from afar!"

While the man boasted and challenged, Sean, without taking his eyes off his attacker, tossed the pistol aside and stood, hands empty and arms spread, and laughed at the warrior before him.

The warrior crouched, eyes squinting, mouth snarling as he grabbed the knife at his waist with his right hand, clasped a tomahawk with his left, lifted his face to the night sky and screamed his war cry. He growled as he charged toward the white man. Sean quickly slipped the Bowie from the scabbard at his back and snatched the tomahawk at his belt to take a stance, feet apart, slightly crouched, and rose to his toes as Eagle lunged forward.

The Indian lifted the hawk high and brought it down as he leaned into his charge, expecting to end the fight with one quick blow, but the blade caught nothing but air, and Sean's razor-sharp Bowie brought blood from a long gash the length of Eagle's forearm. Eagle thrust the knife at Sean's belly, but he stepped back, turning sideways. Blue Eagle was off balance and Sean kicked his foot out from under him, making him fall on his face. It would have been an easy move for Sean to bring his hawk down and split the Indian's back with one blow, but he stepped back instead.

Blue Eagle scrambled to his feet, turned toward Sean, growling as he took the fighter's crouch and the two adversaries began to circle one another. Sean grinned and shook his head, "I was right; you are a blue-bird, no talons, no fangs!"

Sean watched every motion, every move; keeping his eyes on the warriors knowing they would be the give-away of the man's movements. Eagle held his knife, edge up and moved it side to side, eyes squinting as he moved the tomahawk in the same way. Suddenly, he feinted a lunge, and when Sean stepped back, Eagle brought the hawk down just as Sean twisted. It was a glancing blow on his shoulder but caused him to go to one knee. Eagle screamed and lunged, knife extended in a sweeping motion that struck the uplifted hawk of Sean. With the snarl of a wolf and the force of all his strength, Sean gritted his teeth and pushed the knife away. But at the same time swept his knife across the midriff of Eagle, cutting through his tunic and bringing blood. When Eagle pulled back, Sean came to his feet and moved away.

The blood from the cut on Eagle's arm ran down across the back of his hand and into his palm, making it difficult for him to grip the knife. He moved his left arm across his stomach, looked down and saw the blood on his forearm. He looked up at Sean, surprise and anger showing in his eyes. Both men knew Eagle had to strike a death blow, before he was weakened with the loss of blood.

Sean had yet to be bloodied, and circled to the left, countering the moves of Eagle, but the man did not falter. He hunkered lower, reminding Sean of an attacking wolverine, low to the ground and intent on his attack. Eagle screamed, raised his hawk and charged, but Sean was watching the knife, ducking under the uplifted hawk, bringing his own tomahawk down on the bloody arm with the knife. He felt the bone give under the blow, drove his shoulder into the man's chest, knocking him to his knees. Sean stepped forward with the Bowie, put it to the man's throat and pushed him back.

Large frightened eyes stared up at Sean as he pushed the warrior back. Blue Eagle's left arm hung, bent behind the wrist, blood dripping to the ground. His fingers clasped the hawk, but Sean stepped on the flat side of the blade, wrenching it from Eagle's hand. The man was defenseless, and Sean had every right to thrust the knife into the man's throat, but he suddenly brought his hawk up, striking Eagle above his ear with the flat side of the blade, knocking him to the ground, unconscious.

Sean stepped back, sheathed his knife behind his neck, slipped the hawk behind his belt and slowly walked to his horse, picking up his pistol on the way. No one moved or spoke as they watched this white man walk away. He grabbed Dusty's rein, stepped into the stirrup and swung his leg over the cantle. With one look back at the crowd, he gigged the horse forward, brought the grey's lead rope taut and rode from the village.

The moon, now full, shone bright in the garden of stars just over his right shoulder. He searched the sky for the North Star, pointed at it and brought his arm down to a shadowy landmark, and spoke to Indy, "Well, here we are again boy. Just you, me and the horses. By the way, where were you when that fella was tryin' to gut me?" The big wolf turned his head to look up at his friend, opened his mouth and appeared to roll his eyes, then turned toward the trail before them, stretching into his long lazy lope to scout ahead.

CHAPTER TWELVE
COMPANY

THE ESCAPADES OF THE NOCTURNAL CREATURES BROKE THE
monotony of the nighttime travel for Sean. To watch the
big-footed jackrabbits scamper through the sage and
buffalo grass to escape from the coyotes and foxes only to
be plucked from the brink of his hole by the quiet descent
of an eagle told the story of one of life's futilities. Sean
shook his head at the thought and listened to the night
sounds he had come to enjoy. The cry of the nighthawk,
the clatter of the cicadas, and the lovesick bark of the
coyote provided the accompaniment to the shuffling of
the horses' hooves in the sandy soil beneath.

He thought back on his fight with Blue Eagle,
rehashing his moves and the outcome. He remembered
the many times when his family visited the Comanche,
Ute, and Arapaho, and at each village the times he spent
with other youth in the many war games used by the
natives to teach their young how to fight. Whenever they
would wrestle or go to it one on one, they always used
carved imitations of knives and tomahawks, but most

often fought open-handed. Each band had its unique ways of individual combat, and Sean had always done well in the contests. His physique and intelligence had served him well and his quick reflexes often turned the bouts to his favor. Those contests of boys at play had taught him skills that helped him in life.

The silvery glow of the moonlight showed the shadowy hills in the distance. Sean lifted his eyes to the moon, now above his left shoulder and starting its slow descent to the western hills. He calculated he had about two hours before the stars blew out their lanterns and the morning sun chased the moon from the sky. By daylight, he wanted to be settled into a well-protected camp and ready to catch up on his sleep. The comfortable shuffling gait of the horses could easily lull him to sleep in the saddle, but he couldn't allow himself to drop his guard. He knew he was somewhere between the Brulé and the Oglala, neither of which would be very welcoming of an unknown intruder. After his set-to with Blue Eagle, he probably wouldn't be welcome in that camp nor any other camp of the Brulé. But he had taken the job as scout for the army, and he had to know where the camps of the natives were, and if possible, what they might be doing about the settlers moving through or even the other tribes or any other mischief they might be up to.

Sean looked down at Indy, now loping alongside Dusty, "You know boy, takin' this job to find out things is kinda confusing. I don't know what I'm supposed to know and probably won't know it when I know it! And if I try too hard to find out what I'm supposed to know, it might be the last thing I ever know! I guess I just don't know how I'm gonna find out what I need to know!" Indy didn't miss a step, nor did he turn at the senseless rambling of the man in the saddle. Dusty, however, did turn his head back to look at Sean and bobbed his head as he shuffled along.

The long, low, flat-top butte was marked by deep ravines and gullies that cut from the top to the valley floor. Timber darkened the draws and beckoned to Sean as a good place to hide out during the daylight hours. With the tall grass at the mouth of those ravines, there had to be water, and where there was water, he could have coffee. He pushed into a steep-sided draw, weaving through the juniper and cedar, and at the first clearing, or rather a bare shoulder of a finger ridge, he found the thin trickle of a spring with a pool of water twice the size of his hat. Just enough to dip his coffee pot in for that longed-for brew before he turned to his blankets.

When he snuffed out the fire and sat the half-empty pot beside the rock, the long shadows were inching back towards his camp. The sun had risen, and the cloudless sky promised a quiet day for the weary man as he rolled into his blankets at the base of the pungent smelling cedar. Indy lay beside him, and if needed, both could see the mouth of the ravine below. Sean was content, and was soon sound asleep.

But Sean was a light sleeper and often stirred at the movement of the horses or their munching of the grass or when they blew. The familiar sounds were comforting, but their absence could be alarming. Whenever he woke, he would look first to Indy, and if he was not near, then he looked to the horses. If their heads were up, ears pricked, and eyes watchful, something or someone could be approaching. Yet the animals were always quick to recognize that which was familiar and non-threatening and would pay little attention and show no alarm. It was the smell of smoke that woke Sean. He lay unmoving, hand clasping the grip of the pistol, and slowly moved his eyes for the source of the smoke. Maybe it was someone camped nearby, over the ridge maybe, and the breeze carried the smoke in his direction. Then he heard movement, close by, and with a quick glance, he saw Indy was gone. He slowly turned his head toward the juniper near where he had his fire earlier. Someone was bending over the fire, but he quickly recognized the figure. There was no mistaking the taut stretched buckskin tunic and the fringed leggings.

He sat up and smiled at the woman at the fire. It was a small cookfire with a rabbit on a spit above the flames. The coffee pot was at the edge of the coals, and she slowly turned, smiling. Her long hair hung over her shoulders, and she pushed it behind her ear, "You must have been tired," she said as she stood and turned toward him.

"White Fox, what are you doing here?" asked Sean, trying to be stern but failing. He was pleased to see her, and her presence brought a joy he hadn't expected.

"I told you I liked being with you, is that not enough?"

He smiled broadly as he pushed the blankets aside and stood. He walked to her, put his hands at her waist and looked down into the dark eyes, "That's enough for me, but what about your father. I don't imagine he's too happy about you leaving."

"He respects you, Bear Chaser, and when I told him you were going to the Oglala, he said they would kill you. I said that if I go with you, they will not kill you. He did not answer, and he did not stop me."

Sean dropped his eyes to the roasting rabbit, looked beside the fire at an unstrung bow and a quiver of arrows. The rustle of feet beyond the trees told him she had tethered her horse with the others, but when a flash of color came from the trees, he stepped back, looked at Fox and back to a cavorting colt that was jumping and kicking his heels in the air as he ran back and forth to his tethered mother. The two had similar marking with splashes of white and the deep brown of their bay colors. Black manes and tails completed the similarities. Sean looked at a smiling Fox as she answered, "I couldn't leave him behind without his mother!"

He shook his head, squatted on his heels and reached for the coffee pot and a cup. "Looks like your rabbit is 'bout ready!"

She lifted the skewered rabbit and lay it on a plate, tearing it into portions. She handed a plate with the two hindquarters to Sean, scratched at the coals and extracted several roasted yampa roots, placed two on Sean's plate, then sat back to enjoy the bounty.

As he ate, Sean considered. He knew traveling by himself, he was naturally observant and vigilant, but with another, those defenses were lessened. Although there would be two sets of eyes watching for trouble, both would be distracted by the other. But she was probably right about trying to enter the Oglala village. It wouldn't be the same as when he brought the travois of buffalo meat to the Brulé camp. And with Fox already there to tell of her encounter with wolves and with her recognizing Indy, he was made welcome in their camp. But from all he had heard about the Oglala, approaching their camp might be considerably more dangerous.

He finished his meal, sat the plate aside and reached for the coffee cup. He looked at Fox, "Well, this proves you're pretty good with a bow, but have you ever shot a rifle?"

"Yes, I shot my father's rifle one time. But I did not have my own."

"Hmmm, well, let's go up there," he nodded toward the top of the flat butte, "and we'll take a look-see for anybody here 'bouts, and if we're alone, then we'll see if you can learn about usin' a rifle."

"I would like that."

Sean stood, walked to his gear and grabbed the brass telescope, motioned for Fox to follow, and they walked through the trees to the top of the butte. At the crest, they hunkered down on all fours and worked their way to a cluster of rocks. Using the boulders for cover and to rest his elbows, he began scanning the countryside. After his first scan, he handed the scope to Fox and watched as she was surprised at what she saw, then continued to look all around. He enjoyed her wide grin and quiet sounds of wonder.

When she lowered the scope and looked at Sean, she said, "That is wonderful! To be able to see so far!"

"Ummhumm, but did you see anyone?"

"I saw some buffalo, a coyote, and a fox," she declared emphatically, proud of herself.

"Well, then, let's go try your hand at using a rifle. I think you'll find this one is a little different than the one your father had."

Within moments they were back at their camp and Sean grabbed his possibles pouch and the Sharps rifle. As they walked to the end of the shoulder ridge, Sean explained and demonstrated the loading of the rifle with the paper cartridge and a percussion cap. They were back in the trees a little, but the field of fire showed a lightning struck tree with a snag of a stump that was bare of bark. Sean pointed to their target, which stood about a hundred fifty yards away.

Fox looked at the stump, scowled as she looked back at Sean, "But it's so far!" she declared incredulously.

"Not so much. That rifle can shoot," and he paused to look farther across the valley at a rocky promontory at the end of a talus slope, "see those rocks across the valley?"

"Yes, but . . . "

"Yes, that rifle can shoot that far and kill an elk in the doing of it!"

She looked at Sean, down at the rifle, and said, "I will shoot it!"

Sean demonstrated how to shoot from one knee, using the other as a rest for the supporting elbow, and how to sight down the barrel with the front and rear sights. She took the position, held the rifle as he instructed and looked at Sean for more instructions.

"Now, there's two triggers. As you get ready, you'll use the rear trigger and your thumb on the hammer to cock it, like this," and he demonstrated. "Then snug it up to your shoulder, lay your cheek on the stock and take aim. When you're ready, take in a breath, let part out, then slowly squeeze the small front trigger."

Sean stepped back a pace, and watched as she carefully did as instructed. When the big rifle roared, the recoil pushed her back as the muzzle lifted, but she held firm and let a gasp out, but looked to see through the smoke as to where she hit. Sean had watched carefully, and he said,

"You hit it dead center! Look at that chunk you knocked out of that stump!"

She grinned, looking up at Sean and said, "Can I shoot at that?" pointing to the rocks at the talus. The end of the talus was over four hundred yards distant but well within the range of the rifle and Sean grinned as he nodded his head. He handed her a cartridge and a cap, watched as she lowered the lever dropping the falling block, inserted the cartridge and drew the lever up. She pulled back the hammer to place a cap and took her position again. Sean watched, pleased that she needed no additional instruction and just before she pulled the trigger, he used the scope to view the rocks. He said, "There's a light-colored rock near the top of the pile. Aim for that."

The big Sharps boomed, and Sean saw the rock break and tumble from the stack. He chuckled and looked down at Fox, smiled, "You're a natural!"

CHAPTER THIRTEEN
OGLALA

IT WAS A DRY LAND, THE MUTED COLORS OF MOONLIGHT showing little variance in tone, but Sean knew the pale greens of spring still painted the low rolling hills. The soft-edged shadows marked the contours of the land, and the scattered sage and greasewood gave little contrast to variegated flats. The quiet of the early morning hours seemed quieter still with the motionless plains. A silhouette of broad shoulders stood, inviting the weary travelers and they hoped there would be cool water, enticing cover, and a safe refuge, at least for a day.

Night sounds carry and the knowing Fox spoke in soft tones, "Those are called Old Woman Hills, there is a stream that is called Old Woman Creek." She pointed to the obscure mesas off to their right.

"Well, if there's any trees near, that'd be where they are. Looks as good a place as any, and I'm gettin' so hungry, my belly button's pinchin' muh backbone!" answered Sean, keeping his voice low as well.

Fox shook her head as she grinned, "I guess that means you're hungry?"

"Ummhumm, that it do!"

"I know a place," said Fox as she leaned forward to kick her paint filly into a trot, the colt kicking up his heels to follow. When she rounded a shoulder of the mesa, she disappeared, but Sean willingly followed, wondering where she was leading them. She sat smiling, leaning on the withers of the paint, and with a sweeping gesture, motioned to a horseshoe-shaped basin tucked into the side of the mesa. The chuckle of water told of a live stream and the indistinguishable figures at the foot of the slopes promised ample tree cover.

"My village spent one summer here, this was my favorite place to get away," she explained as she slid from atop the paint. The mare and colt followed Fox as she started into the basin, picking up firewood as she walked between the trees.

Sean stepped down, stretched his legs and bent backwards to stretch his back; it had been a long night, the second one on the trail with Fox. She offered to take the lead since she had a reasonably good idea about where the Oglala were camped. With spring in full sway and summer coming, she explained they would be getting ready to make their trek to Fort Laramie for the yearly allotment of goods according to the treaty of 1851. But she also added they had seldom received all the goods as promised but the people would also use the time to make trades with the others at both Fort Laramie and Bernard.

When he stepped through the trees, she stood before him, hands on hips, and smiling. She stretched her arms out and pirouetted as she asked, "Do you like it? This was my special place!" The grass-covered clearing was on a wide flat shoulder, surrounded by juniper, and offered ample space for all their needs. The protection was excellent with the slopes of the basin rising to the mesa tops three to four hundred feet above the valley floor. With the basin and the slopes sparsely covered with juniper, piñon, and cedar, their presence was well hidden.

Sean grinned as he looked at the enthusiastic Fox, "Yes, it is perfect." He dropped his eyes and added, "I'll strip the horses and then get some more firewood. Then I want to take a last look around from up on top there. By the time we get there, the sun should be up enough so we can see."

The brilliant glow of gold lit the eastern horizon as the couple found a seat on a wide expanse of lichen-covered rock sitting between a pair of gnarled cedar. The trees were enough to break up their silhouette and mask their presence from anyone in the wide valley below. As the long shadows slowly crawled back to their source, Sean's attention was focused well to their north. He had followed the waterway in the valley bottom, that was carved by the winding Old Woman Creek, beyond the confluence with the creek just below and the second stream that came from the hills. He couldn't make it out, but he was certain he saw movement. He dropped the glass as he turned to Fox, "I think I saw some movement way up there beyond Old Woman Creek. Take a look."

Fox accepted the scope, stretched out to look, and turned back to Sean, "They are too far to tell, but that is the direction of the camp of Wašičuŋ Tȟašúŋke, *He-Has-A-White-Man's-Horse*, the chief of the Oglala. Their winter camp is south of the Paha Sapa, what your people call the Black Hills."

Sean accepted the telescope and looked again, "That's a good half day's travel from here. We can have somethin' to eat, maybe get a little rest, and they'll be near enough to make sure." He rolled to his side, looked to Fox and grinned, "So, what's for breakfast?"

THE CARAVAN of the Oglala stretched out more than a mile as the village trudged past the mouth of the valley where Sean and Fox were camped. From atop the mesa, they watched, trying to determine if this was the band of Wašičuŋ Tȟašúŋke. As the line of people plodded by, Sean tried to estimate the number of lodges. He started by counting the many travois, but soon lost count and guessed there were well over sixty lodges, making the number of the village to be close to two hundred, with at least seventy-five or more warriors. This was a strong band and would be capable of exerting their will on any size of wagon train or fort, especially since so many soldiers had been called to the east for the war.

"These are Oglala, and I believe they are of the Wagluhe band. That is the band of Horse," stated Fox.

"How many bands of Oglala are there?" asked Sean, continuing to watch the passers-by through his scope.

"Seven, but I do not believe this is all the Wagluhe. They have more warriors than those. They might be on a hunt or . . ."

Sean sat back near the tree, looking at Fox. "Seven bands? Are they all about the same size?"

"Yes, some more, some less. But mostly."

Sean shook his head as he quickly calculated, *Seven bands, a hundred warriors each, and that's just the Oglala,*

*there's still the Brulé, the Miniconjou, and others. That's thou-
sands of warriors!* He briefly considered the presumptuous
attitude of the politicians and others that had no concept
of what could happen if all these united against the white
man. With so many trying to cheat on the annuities, break
treaties on territory boundaries, and more, it seemed to
him there was nothing but trouble waiting.

"Do you think I could meet with this man, the chief,
you said his name was He-Has-a-White-Man's-Horse?"

Fox considered, knowing that was what Sean had
planned to do even though it could mean his life. "Horse
and my father, Crow Dog, are friends. I might convince
him to speak to you. But he will not stop while they are
traveling."

"If they're goin' to Laramie, then we'll just catch up to
them there. For now, do you know where we might find
the Miniconjou?"

Fox looked at Sean, trying to understand what this
white man was doing that he wanted to meet with the
different bands of the Lakota people. But she believed he
was a good man and did not mean bad to her people,
although she could not fully understand. She spoke softly
when she replied, "They often camp in the Paha Sapa, the
Black Hills, as you call them."

"Would they make the journey to Fort Laramie like the
others?"

"They have, but not always. Their chief, Hewáŋžiča,
One Horn, has been friendly with the whites, but he does
not trust them. He says they lie. He has been chief a long
time and is a strong leader."

"Then maybe we'll see if we can meet with him before
going back to Laramie." He stepped back into the trees,

paused and turned back to Fox. "I need to get to know these people better, they have been lied to many times and the leaders of the military and others have no respect for them, and I think it's because they haven't taken the time to get to know them." They walked side by side as Sean continued, "I want to help these people and the whites to somehow trust each other and to live together peaceably, but I'm not sure if I can do much.

"I was raised with different native peoples as our friends. My father's first real friend among the native people was a Shaman with the Comanche, her name was White Feather. And as a youngster, the only friends I knew were among the Comanche, the Ute, and the Arapaho. We respected and often helped one another. There were even times when my father fought alongside warriors of these people. But there are those among all people that do wrong and lie and steal from others. That's what we have to overcome. So, I'm hoping that if I meet and learn about these leaders and their people, maybe something can be done."

Fox smiled as she listened to this man that had become her friend and perhaps more. He was good and what he wanted was more than she hoped. Crow Dog, her father, had told her to learn from this man and to always protect the people.

She led out as they took to a trail that paralleled that path that had been traveled by the Oglala, but they were bound to the northeast to find the land of the Miniconjou. As they traveled, Sean asked, "Tell me more about the bands of the Lakota."

Fox continued with Sean's education regarding the Sioux, focusing first on the Oglala. "The father of Horse is

Old Chief Smoke, who is a Shirt Wearer, that is one who is a leader from the *Ogle Tanka Un* warrior society that directs their people in all things of their village lives. It is a great honor to be a Shirt Wearer. The Old Chief Smoke made the camp of his people by Fort Laramie. That is how they became known as the Wagluhe, or Loafers, those who lived with their wives' relatives, because they lived by the fort. When more soldiers came to the fort, Chief Smoke moved his people away, but he has been a friend to the whites and has tried to make peace among his people."

"Then why did you think my life would in danger if I approached his camp?"

"Wašičuŋ Tȟašúŋke, or Horse, is the son of Old Chief Smoke, and he is now the leader of the village. The warriors around him would not want you to approach him; they would kill anyone they did not know. That is their duty, to protect the chief."

CHAPTER FOURTEEN
VILLAGE

WITH ONLY TWO STOPS TO REST THE HORSES AND TO TAKE A bit of food for themselves, it had been a long night's travel. Although they journeyed east, they had crossed a lot of rugged and desolate land. Even the night sounds seemed to be dimmed or even absent and the nocturnal creatures that had always been company, were nowhere to be seen. Only one stop had given them any water, and the canteens had been stuffed into the bedrolls to keep from making their hollow and obnoxious sounds as they bounced their empty shells on the saddle. When Sean saw the moonlight reflect an invitation from the creek beyond the shadowy line of willows, he cast his vote for a stop.

"Yes, our horses need water, and there is grass for them, but if we stay here, we will be seen. There," she pointed further east, "is water and cover where we can camp and not be seen." Sean looked to the silhouetted horizon that showed the jagged edge of mountains. Although these were not like the western peaks, they showed the familiar contours and heights that told they were near the Paha Sapa.

It was about a half-hour later when Fox turned into the mouth of a canyon that cradled a small creek in the bottom. The sides of the canyon were covered with juniper and piñon, but the table-top buttes above were bare. The campsite met their needs, and a small fire was soon sharing its heat with the sweaty coffee pot. The pre-dawn light filtered through the juniper branches that promised to keep the smoke well-hidden, at least until the coffee was ready, although their Johnny cakes, laying on the flat rock beside the fire, did little to absorb the heat.

"Today, I will find some other foods, there are roots that are very good, and some berries are ready. Perhaps you will find us some meat," suggested Fox, smiling at Sean, knowing he would not hunt until dusk.

"How close are we to the Miniconjou camp?" he asked.

"We are close. When there is light, you may see their smoke from up there," she pointed with her chin to the high point of the ridge above them.

He turned to look at the dimly lit slope behind him, seeing the top edge catch a bit of the light of the promised dawn. He guessed it to be about two to three hundred feet higher than their camp, giving them good cover to the south and east. The narrow valley opened to the north with another wider valley at the bottom, also holding a stream that could be heard from across the valley floor. He looked back at Fox, "So, tell me a little more about the Miniconjou," he suggested as he reached for the offered cup of coffee.

After pouring herself a cup of the brew she had grown to like, she sat back and began. "One Horn is old, but strong. He was known for his bravery in battle and his many achievements as a hunter. Stories have been told about how, as a young man, before his people had many horses, he could run down a buffalo and drive his arrow into the heart. No one else could do that, although many tried. When the villages met together for the Sun Dance, they would have contests and races, and he always took the prize. His band is called the *Wakpokinyan* or Flies Along the Stream people. And he has two sons, Spotted Elk and Touch the Clouds." She paused, dropping her head as she smiled at a remembrance.

Sean noticed her expression and asked, "What about the sons?" with a skeptical tone.

"Touch the Clouds and I were friends when our camps joined for the Dance," she smiled coyly as she dropped her eyes.

"Just how many of these fellas am I going to have to fight, anyway?"

Fox leaned forward, stretching out her hand toward Sean as she quickly answered, "Oh no, no, no more," in a tone that showed genuine concern.

Sean took advantage of the moment, folded his arms across his chest and said sternly, "Better not! A man can only take so much, ya know." But his stern expression broke into a smile as he looked at the fearful eyes of Fox. When she saw his smile, she breathed deep and sat back, a bit of a grin showing on her face.

Sean finished his coffee, threw the dregs at the base of the tree, and stood to kick dirt onto the coals of the fire. He tossed a Johnny Cake to Fox, took the other and began munching on it as he went to the saddle bags for the scope. Once atop the ridge, they began their search for any sign of the village. It wasn't until the first rays of the morning sun bent their way down to stretch across the flats that they spotted the wispy streams of cookfire smoke lifting their way to a cloudless sky.

Less than a mile to the north, the river had carved its way through the low hills, leaving a steep-sided canyon with a wide alluvial plain in the bend of the river where the village lay. Although from their vantage point, the lodges of the village were not visible, the large horse herd was grazing contentedly in the tall grass at the mouth of the canyon.

Fox turned to Sean with a satisfied smile, "There is the village."

"Should we scout it out, or just ride right in?" asked Sean, realizing he was surrendering his choices to Fox. His pa had often told him that when you travel alone you are more vigilant and careful, and all the choices are yours. But when you are with someone, too often your defenses are lessened, and you're less decisive. But Sean believed he was simply yielding to her experience and knowledge of the people and their ways. It was his own thinking that a man that learns from others and uses their knowledge to supplement his own, is the smarter for it.

"To show you are not afraid, we should ride in, but without weapons."

"You mean leave our rifles behind?"

"No, I mean without weapons in your hands. I will speak to them, to tell who we are and why we are entering their camp. There may be young warriors that try to count coup to test you, but you cannot turn on them."

"Yeah, that happened in your camp. Course, I had to fight my way out too," he declared, remembering the fight with Blue Eagle. "Am I gonna have to fight my way out of this camp by takin' on another of your old boyfriends again?"

She frowned, looking at Sean with a question, "What is boy-friend?"

"A boyfriend is someone that want to be with you and no one else. And he wants you to feel the same way about him. Like Blue Eagle."

"Are you my boyfriend?" she asked, with her head slightly ducked as she looked from under the thin black eyebrows, her dark eyes shining and a slight smile on her lips.

"Uh, uh, well, maybe," he stammered as he felt his heart beating a little faster, but not knowing if it was from fear or excitement or the uncertainty of the moment.

She lifted her eyes and smiled broadly, "Yes, you are my boyfriend," she declared, leaving no room for argument. "We will go to the village after mid-day," she announced as she started back to the path that led to their camp. Sean stood and followed in the same manner that men have followed their women for eons, uncertain about what was happening, but hopeful, nevertheless.

With the horses grazing on the deep grass and the rising sun warming the slopes, the duo were soon comfortable on their blankets and getting the much-needed rest after the long night's travel. Indy lay between the two with his head on the outstretched arm of Sean and the horses, tethered nearby gave the comfortable cadence of their munching as the lullaby for the pair. It was the high-pitched whistle from a nearby prairie dog village that brought Sean awake, the furry pig of the prairie sounding its alarm of a predator among them.

Sean lay still, looking at the quiet form of Indy at the crook of his arm, then to the horses that showed no alarm. When he looked back, Fox was looking at him, wide eyes showing emotion but no fear. As he looked at the shadows, he knew it was just past mid-day and whispered to Fox, "Bout time for us to go to the village."

She smiled, sat up and began packing up their gear. Sean fetched the horses, saddling the dapple-grey with the pack-saddle first, then started on the others. When he was finished gearing up the horses, Fox had the paniers loaded and ready. Before they stepped aboard, Sean took Fox's hand in his and bowed his head for a quick prayer for their safety. As he lifted his concluded, he looked into the smiling eyes of Fox who said, "Let us go, boyfriend!"

CHAPTER FIFTEEN
MINICONJOU

THEY WERE FOLLOWED BY FOUR WARRIORS THAT CAME FROM the horse herd; each man had a lance or a war club and stayed near, watching the visitors. Sean and Fox rode side by side, Indy between their horses and slightly ahead, as if he was the leader. Sean detected a difference in attitude among these villagers. When he entered the camp of the Brulé, the people held back, suspicious and untrusting, but these showed only curiosity. When they saw the big wolf, most would step back and point out the animal to others. Some approached with uplifted hands to touch or greet the newcomers, expressions showed friendliness, and no one ran for their weapons.

As they neared the central compound, an old man stepped in front of them, looked down at the wolf and held his hand up for them to stop. Indy was no more than two paces from the man, but at the soft-spoken command of Sean, he dropped to his belly to wait, watching the old man before them.

"Why do you come to our village?" The question came

from a raspy voice but one that carried authority. The old man looked from Sean to Fox, and Fox answered, "We come in peace to speak to Hewáŋžiča. I am White Fox, my father is Crow Dog of the Brulé," then motioning to Sean, "This is Bear Chaser of the Arapaho."

"Why do you come?" repeated the man, looking at Sean.

"To learn of your people and learn of peace. I am told your chief, One Horn, is a great and wise leader. There is much we can learn from him," answered Sean.

"I am Etokeah," and with a simple hand motion, he directed them to step down from their horses and wait.

The old man had long grey hair in braids over both shoulders, wearing a long, fringed tunic shirt decorated with scalp locks, beads, and elk's teeth, turned away and started for the big lodge behind him. He stood beside the entry flap and spoke, loud enough to be heard but not understood, and the flap was thrown back, and a very dignified but older warrior stepped from the lodge. He had a commanding presence and austere expression. But his appearance was different from the others in that he had very long hair, grey and white, twisted together into two long parts and both piled high atop his head, giving the appearance he was wearing a hair bonnet. His tunic was decorated in a bold geometric pattern of blue, white, and yellow beads that covered both shoulders and much of his chest. Long fringe hung from the sleeves, tail, and yokes. Most impressive was the number of scalp locks and porcupine quills that hung from the shoulders, sleeves, and the rest of the tunic. What caught Sean's eye was an out-of-place shell that was held at his throat with a fine braided hair band. The shell was alabaster and apparently came from the ocean as nothing resembling it could be found in the plains or mountains.

One Horn stepped before the visitors with arms folded across his chest as he looked at the intruders to his village. He looked past Sean and Fox to Indy, still lying between the horses, and back at the two before him. He looked Sean up and down then to Fox, "You are Lakota, you say he is Arapaho?"

"He has lived with the Arapaho and others; he is now a scout with Fort Laramie," she answered.

One Horn looked again at Sean, "Why are you here?"

"To learn of your people, to learn from you the ways of peace."

The chief looked long and hard at the white man before him, these were words he had never heard from one of his kind, and he was skeptical that one so young could speak with this wisdom. "We will talk of this. The council will meet with you after the sun rises," as he spoke, he also used the sign language to be certain he was understood.

Sean answered in the same way, speaking in Lakota and sign, "It is good."

With a nod, he turned back to his lodge and Etokeah, or Hump, motioned for them to follow. They were led to an empty lodge near the edge of the camp close to the stream. Hump motioned, "This is your lodge as you are with us."

As Hump turned to leave, Sean stopped him with, "Will you or someone tell us when we are to meet with One Horn?"

"Yes," responded Hump with no further explanation as he left.

Sean looked to Fox, "Talkative bunch, aren't they?" he said as he started stripping the horses of their gear.

"Many words are not the same as wisdom."

Sean paused, turned to look at Fox who had busied herself preparing the ring of stones for the cook fire, thought about what she said, and with a shrug and uplifted eyebrows, returned to his work. As he stacked the gear, he thought about what had happened in the past several days. First the visit with the Brulé, then seeing the Oglala and now with the Miniconjou. He wondered if he was a little out of his element talking with the chiefs of these great nations. He was hopeful of learning something, anything, that might help the different people to live in peace. The pleasant memories of his childhood and the times spent with the different tribes that did not fight with one another and had been peaceful with the whites had given him enough optimism to continue his efforts. But many things had changed as he grew older, even the land of his youth had become one of conflict with the Ute allying with the Apache, the Comanche with the Kiowa, and the Crow, Shoshoni, and Arapaho not only allying themselves with other tribes, but most resisting the advance of the white man. Maybe he was too hopeful, or at least too poorly equipped, about doing his part to try to bring peace to the plains.

But the memories of his pa saying, "Remember son, no matter what you get into, as long as you do your best, there's no job too big for you and none you can't handle. Sure, you might get a few scraped knuckles, shed a little blood, but if you're in the right, don't let anyone or anything keep you from doing the job!"

He plopped down on the ground next to Indy, absentmindedly running his hand through the thick fur at the wolf's neck, and as he sat cross-legged, he stared at the tiny flames licking at the fresh wood placed there by Fox. She looked at the morose man, "Why are you angry?"

Her words startled him to attention, he thought about what she said, and asked, "Angry? I'm not angry."

"You look angry. What is it that has you so..."

And before she could finish the question, Sean interrupted, "Just thinkin' too much, I reckon." He stood, looking around at the camp, "This is a mighty big camp. Ain't never seen one this size before. And the people, they seem a lot friendlier, don'tchu think?"

"Yes. But it is always so when there is a strong leader that knows no fear. One Horn has always shown his people the way to treat others. He is a mighty warrior and those that have known him as their enemy are fearful of him, but he is also a wise man and leads his people in great ways."

"You know, I've seen that just about everywhere, among other tribes and even the white man. When the leader is a good man, the people with him will be like him. I've seen that with leaders of wagon trains, commanders of military forts, chiefs of villages. People follow the example of those that lead, whether good or bad. Too bad more leaders don't understand that."

"Yes, and I have also seen times when someone who is not the leader, can show the leader how to be good and do the right thing. Is not that what you want to do?"

"I s'pose so, but how do I get those that are the chiefs to listen?" answered Sean, still a little wistful.

"Perhaps you must take it to *Wakan Tanka*, or your God, and let Him show you what to do."

Sean looked up at a smiling Fox, stood, and walked to her, slipping his hands to her waist and drawing her close. He looked into her dark eyes that showed a hint of humor, "You are just exactly what I need," and they embraced.

HE SAT at the edge of the flat-top butte above the camp when the first band of grey parted the horizon from the darkness. The stars dimmed and the waning moon hung just above the western hills, as Sean communed with his Lord. He had just concluded his prayer and looked at the village below, estimating there were well over a hundred lodges. He heard the rattle of stones that caused Indy to come to his feet, but as the wolf recognized Fox, he dropped back to his belly beside Sean. Fox came to his side, sat down next to him and asked, "Would you like something to eat before you meet with the council?"

"Coffee's all. I was a little restless last night, been up here since early mornin'."

"I know. You must know that One Horn honors you to have you meet with the council. I believe he will listen to anyone that might help bring peace."

"But I didn't come to talk, I came to listen and learn," replied Sean, showing his frustration.

"Before they talk, they will listen. What you say will show them if you will listen. If you try to tell them what to do, that will also tell them you do not want to listen."

He looked at the woman at his side, wondering about her wisdom. It wasn't just that she knew about the Sioux; she knew about the leaders of the people and their ways and the manner they dealt with others. But more than that, she seemed to see inside a person, what they really were and what they could be, and more.

"Can you come with me?" asked a hopeful Sean.

"It is not my place. I am a warrior among my people, but I have chosen to be at your side. They do not want to hear from another Lakota, they want to hear from you, a white man and a man of the fort."

He dropped his head, breathed deep, and looked back to Fox. "Then, I guess we better go back down and have that coffee before they send for me."

CHAPTER SIXTEEN
COUNCIL

ALL THE COUNCIL WAS SEATED WHEN SEAN WAS ALLOWED to enter the lodge. With a fire circle in the center, several of the elders and chiefs were seated in a semi-circle to the left of the entry. Sean was motioned to sit opposite the leaders, close to the fire ring. Others were seated near the back of the lodge in the semi-darkness, and Sean could not discern the number of warriors present. One Horn sat slightly closer to the ring than the others, but the war chiefs and elders were assembled on both sides of the chief and facing Sean. To his right sat Hump and the others, five in all, whose names Sean would learn later, were on either side.

One Horn began, "We asked why you came to our village, you said to learn of peace. Now, tell us who you are and why we should hear you and let you learn of our ways." No one else moved or spoke as the chief looked to Sean and waited for him to speak.

Sean took a deep breath that lifted his shoulders, then, forcing himself to relax, he began, "I am known as Bear

Chaser among the Arapaho, Shoshoni, Ute, and Comanche. My father is Longbow." At the mention of his father's name, some moved and spoke quietly among themselves. When they were silent, Sean continued, "I was asked by the soldier chief, General Harney, to serve as a scout. He suggested I learn from the great Sioux chiefs to know how to help both the whites and the natives. There will be a different soldier chief at Laramie soon, and I am to help him learn of the people of the plains and the mountains. I want to learn the way of peace among the people so our peoples can live without war."

Hump spoke, "Do you come with a white man's paper to make a treaty?"

"No, I do not have that authority. I am not a chief. And I have learned that the other treaties have not worked. Paper means nothing; a man's word should be enough," answered Sean.

Again, there was murmuring among those beside the chief and those behind Sean, but Sean looked only at the chief, waiting for any other comments.

"Did the soldier chief, General Harney, the Butcher, leave the fort?" This question came from one of the war leaders to the left of One Horn, Black Moon.

"Do you know of the white man's war in the east?"

The questioner shook his head, looked to the others, and no one spoke. He looked back to Sean for more.

"The white men fight each other. Those that live in the south are fighting those that live in the north. They fight because they cannot agree about things like territory boundaries, slaves or captives, and those that try to tell others how to live." Sean watched as his words were taken in by the leaders, many nodding their heads in understanding and even agreement. When he spoke about territories, it was a familiar subject to these people that fought against the Assiniboine, Arikara, and Crow about their territories and had for many years. Although their southern territory bordered that of the Cheyenne and Arapaho, they had allied themselves with those people.

"Did all the soldiers leave the fort?" asked another.

"No, just those with the General. There are still soldiers there, and there will be more soon," answered Sean, careful to be truthful but not betray the weakness of the skeleton crew of soldiers left at the fort. He knew if the Sioux were to challenge those few soldiers left, there would be no doubt they could easily take the fort.

"The supplies we were promised, will they come?" asked another, known as Lame Deer.

"I was told they would be at the fort as promised."

"Aiiieeee!" came an outburst from the back, "He lies! Like all white men, he lies!"

Many of those seated behind Sean echoed the cry of the protest, and it was only when One Horn raised his hand that they quieted.

"We have never received all that was promised! Every time we go to the fort, we are told that we get what they have and that not all was there. We were promised powder and lead for our rifles to hunt, but it does not come. We were promised many supplies of food, and they do not come. Every time we go to the fort, they lie to us and say we do not get more! Out village did not go last summer, we do not go this summer!" declared One Horn, angrily glaring at Sean.

Sean kept his eyes on One Horn, never turning away, and answered, "The General told me the supplies would come. If you do not get what is promised, I will do all I can to make it right." He had to stop himself before saying more; although he wanted to promise they would get all they had coming, but he knew with the war in the east, the needed goods might be in short supply.

"If you do not make treaty, how can you get what has been promised?" asked Black Moon.

"I am not a leader; I am not a chief. I can-not make promises. All I can do is try, and I will try to get all you have been promised."

The tone of the council mellowed somewhat, grumbling ceased, and One Horn spoke to Sean, "You want to learn our way of peace? It is this. We do what we say we will do. We expect others to do the same."

When he finished, Black Moon added, "We do not speak for another. We do not tell another what he is to do. When we, as a council, decide what is best for our people, we tell them, and they must decide if they want to do as we do."

Hump spoke, "Our people teach all of our young together. They learn from everyone and gain their own wisdom. We teach them about our people and our past for them to learn respect for those who have gone before."

"Our Shaman teaches of *Wakan Tanka* and shares his wisdom with another to pass it on. We teach our young the skills and wisdom of life, and to respect one another. If they do not learn these things, they must leave the village of the people," said Lame Deer, the second war leader and wearer of the Shirt.

The instruction and teaching continued through most of the morning, but as mid-day approached, the chief lifted his hand, "It is enough." He looked to Sean, "Now you may go to your woman and think about these things. We will talk again, you and me," he motioned to Sean and himself. Then with a simple wave, he dismissed everyone from the lodge, and they filed out quietly.

Once outside, several came to Sean and spoke simple greetings and even encouragement. When he was alone, Sean started toward his lodge, but Hump came alongside and put his hand on Sean's shoulder, "Bear Chaser, it is good that you come to our village. The council has decided to send some of our people to the fort to see if you speak the truth. Perhaps this time we will receive what we were promised."

Sean, Fox, and Indy walked through the camp, speaking with many and often being stopped by youngsters wanting to see the wolf. Indy was especially patient with the little ones and made a big hit with the families. They talked about the villagers, the life of the Sioux, and the possibility of peace.

"As we are here, it seems like it would be so easy to have peace. And when One Horn spoke of the way of the people, that is the way it should be with everyone. But I know there are those, even among the Miniconjou and others, that don't do as the elders say, and they are sent from the village. I've had some experience with renegades like that, and they're no different than those of other tribes or many white men." Sean kicked at a stone as they walked, showing his frustration.

"Is that why the whites are at war with each other?" asked Fox.

He kicked at a small stone, thought a moment, "Well, there's more to it than that, but the issue at the middle of everything is slavery. But there's been slavery among most people since the beginning of time. It's the old story of one people exerting their will over others. Even the Sioux take captives and make them slaves. You were taken from your family, and in many ways, you were no different than a slave. You were kept from your family, made to do what you didn't want to, had to live with those that controlled you. That's the same as slavery," he argued.

"Perhaps. But Crow Dog and his woman, Runs in Water, took me as their own and they became my mother and father."

"Yes, and that happens sometimes with other slaves, but that still doesn't make for peace between people."

They walked together quietly, mulling the shared thoughts and Sean said, "The chief wants us to eat with him and his woman this evening, but I think we will leave tomorrow. I would like to go to the Powder River country, that's supposed to be the territorial border between the Lakota and Crow. Maybe there are other villages we can visit."

"You know the Crow and the Lakota are enemies?" asked Fox, concerned.

"Yes, but I need to see the country, maybe the people, then we will turn back to the south and return to Laramie." He looked at Fox, considering, "Will you come with me? Or do you want to go back to the camp of Crow Dog?"

Fox looked at Sean with a sidelong stare, then letting a smile come slowly; she answered, "We will go to the fort, boyfriend."

CHAPTER SEVENTEEN
POWDER

THE HEADWATERS OF THE POWDER RIVER FOUND THEIR beginnings from the spring runoff, leaving behind sandy bottomed draws that clawed their way across the arid landscape of the plains. Greasewood, sage, yucca, and a variety of cacti pushed at the clumps of buffalo grass and the stretches of blue grama. Rattlesnakes outnumbered the jackrabbits five to one, but the coyotes kept that population under control. The multiple stream-beds held water whenever the heavens dumped their excess, but usually the sandstone banks crumbled upon themselves, leaving little evidence that any moisture was ever found. Hawks, eagles, and a rare osprey could be seen in the blue skies as they circled the many prairie dog villages to see what was on the menu for that day. It was a desolate land.

For the last two days of their journey, their diet had been rabbit, and more rabbit. They made camp on the lee side of a knoll that rose about a hundred feet from the creek bottom. The little stream held the only water for miles and as it twisted back on itself, it had carved out a cutback from the knoll that offered good cover for the day. There was ample graze for the three horses and the bluff would lend a little shade from the afternoon sun, but for now, the sunrise showed only brilliant oranges to color the stunted willows by the creek.

Sean walked back from the stream with full canteens and coffeepot, grinning at Fox's efforts to get a fire started with buffalo chips. Although they had seen sign of the migrating herds, the woolies were long gone by the time Sean and Fox made their crossing. The great herds of bison traveled to the north and the vast grasslands that beckoned their migrations each spring, but those lands were about two days travel farther north from their campsite for the day. As he neared, he saw Fox had used dried cholla cactus with bits of dead greasewood and sage, to have their fire ready for the coffeepot. The stack of buffalo chips would be used once the bed of hot coals could support them. But for now, the almost smokeless fire provided all they needed.

"Come dusk, I'll work along the creek bottom and hopefully find us a deer or even a desert bighorn and get us a little red meat for a change. We've eaten so much rabbit, I had to fight the urge to hop my way back from the creek!"

Fox laughed and giggled as she stirred the fire and said, "I would like to see you hop like a rabbit!"

"If we have to eat any more of that stringy meat, we'll both be hoppin' around!" he declared as he sat down an arm's length from Fox. He looked at the rising sun and at the cloudless sky overhead, "It's gonna be a warm day today. No clouds to offer rain and that ol' sun is shinin' mighty bright. An' I'm thinkin' we ain't gonna see no

Crow anywhere. I haven't seen any sign of anything but buffalo."

Fox nodded her head to indicate the bluff behind them, "There was sign of many horses there, but it was several days old. I think it was the warriors from the Oglala."

Sean scowled as he thought, "Yeah, you did say they were missin' some of their men. How many ya' reckon?"

"Many. Twenty or more. But they had more horses, maybe taken from the Crow."

He looked at her, thinking, remembering, "That Laramie Treaty said the Powder River was the west boundary of the Lakota Territory and both the Crow and the Lakota signed it, but you're sayin' none of 'em abide by it, why?"

"My father said all this land," she gave a sweeping motion indicating the land to the north and west, "was the land of the Lakota. It was not the land of the Crow just because some white men at the fort said. But since that time, the Crow and the Lakota have fought, and most of that land has been taken back. But the Crow still raid in this land as the Lakota raid in their land. Our people, the Brulé, heard the Crow had taken many horses from the Oglala this spring. That is why their warriors had gone into the land they claim, to take the horses and captives back and to show the Crow the Oglala were greater."

He watched her tend the fire and move the coffeepot closer as he thought of the continuing struggle between the Crow and Lakota. Was it not always the way of mankind, one conflict escalates to another, and another? One wrong cries for vengeance and the battle brings death, sorrow, but honor and pride as well. And was it any different with the war now being waged in the east? He thought that God must be sitting in heaven, shaking His head at the selfish stupidity of His creation. The rattle of the coffeepot brought Sean's attention back to the fire.

Fox had ground some coffee beans on the flat rock behind her, and she now dropped a handful into the pot before pushing it back to the coals. She brushed off her hands and sat back, "Will we go further to the west or will we go south to the fort?"

"I'm 'bout ready to turn back to the fort. I'd like to get there 'fore the supply wagons an' they'll be coming in soon. I reckon those Oglala prob'ly run the Crow too far west for us to find a village, so, we'll just start back tonight." He looked to the sky, "It'll be a clear night an' even though the moon's waning, I think we'll see alright, don'tchu?"

"Yes." She looked down at her side, "And my Indy will scout for us."

"*Your* Indy? Since when is he *your* Indy?"

"He saved me, so I am his, and he is mine!" she declared, leaving no room for argument.

Sean chuckled and said, "Pour me a cup of coffee. I'll have to drink on that one!"

THE REST of the morning was spent cleaning rifles, repairing their gear, and lazing about. The morning sun, sans shade, was too warm to make sleep possible, but shortly after mid-day they stretched out in the slim line of shade promised by the bluff behind the campfire. A rattle of stones and the sudden jump of Indy brought Sean instantly awake, but the wolf stood looking at the edge of the bluff and was silent and unmoving. Sean turned to look and saw nothing. Looked to the horses and they were not alarmed. He looked to Indy and asked in a whisper, "What is it boy? What'd you see?" He rubbed the wolf's scruff, and the black leaned into the petting, concerned only about the attention. Sean stood and with pistol in hand, walked to the edge of the bluff, and climbed up to see fresh deer tracks. It was evident a deer had probably come to water, but saw the people and the wolf, spooked, and fled. Sean looked around, satisfied, and returned to the fire circle, felt the coffee-pot, shook his head and poured a cup of tepid java.

The sun had lowered well below the bluff, and the colors of the sunset were painting the flats as Fox rose and came to Sean's side. "What did you see?"

"Just a deer that got spooked and jumped, kicked some rocks as he fled."

"Ummm, a fresh deer steak would taste good for our meal," she suggested.

"I was thinkin' the same thing. I'm gonna take my bow and go looking for one." He stood and walked toward the gear, withdrew his longbow and quiver full of arrows. As he hung the quiver at his side, he stepped into the bow to notch the string and turned with a smile to Fox, "I'm goin' upstream yonder, but I might have to go a ways before I find anything. I should be back 'fore full dark, though."

Fox watched at Sean and Indy traipsed across the flat, staying back from the stream and using the contours of the land to shield his image from the willows. He knew the deer would come from either side of the stream and he was wary of stepping on a rattle-snake that had yet to retreat from sunning himself on the rocks. After about two miles of moving, ducking, hiding, and stalking, all he had to show for his efforts was the memory of the deer tracks back by camp. Dusk was rapidly retreating, and he and the wolf started back. He had seen some jackrabbits and resigned himself to the possibility of more grilled rabbit, if he could bag one on the way back. Luck was with him, and he took two of the long-eared, big-footed furballs. With the rabbits hanging from his quiver, he trudged back to the camp.

When he didn't see the horses, he thought Fox had brought them up to ready them for their night's journey, and he kept on towards the camp. But as he neared, there were no horses. He dropped behind a large sage and looked, but there was nothing. No horses, no packs, no saddles and worse, no Fox! He looked at the terrain, making certain he was at their campsite, and he knew he was not mistaken. Everything was gone!

CHAPTER EIGHTEEN
CROW

SEAN MADE A QUICK SEARCH OF THE CAMP, CHECKING FOR any sign that might have been left by Fox and the tracks of the attackers, anything that would tell him more. Indy stayed by his side, looking at everything as did Sean, smelling, searching, knowing something was wrong. The best Sean could tell, there were eight to ten attackers, Indian, but he could not tell if they were Crow, Lakota, or any other. But he knew he had little time to get White Fox away from her captors before something terrible might happen. He determined the band had left the camp at an easy gait, heading to the north. Dusty and the other two horses were led behind the others, and Sean gritted his teeth. He knew that if anyone tried to ride Dusty, a one-man horse, they would be in for the ride of their life and Dusty would undoubtedly be more dangerous to his captors than a crazed grizzly.

He motioned to Indy, and the two took off in pursuit at a ground-eating trot. Although over great distances a horse can easily out cover more country than a man, but in shorter treks, a man can out-do a horse. But Sean wasn't concerned about what a horse could do or what a man could do; he only knew his commitment. And that was to rescue Fox and let the devil take the high road, because he would get her back and the captors would pay the piper for this dance.

The skirts of darkness covered the land, but the glimmering lanterns of the sky provided enough light for Sean to follow the ghostly black beast that kept his nose to the trail of the kidnappers. A quick glance at the stars told Sean they were moving to the northwest, initially following the streambed until the trail turned away and the churned soil showed the horses had been kicked up to a trot. He kept his pace, what his pa had called a dog-trot, and his long-legged stride kept him close behind Indy. The wolf trotted easily, his blaze-orange eyes piercing the darkness and his deep chest catching every whiff of his familiar horse friends and the woman.

The land rose and fell in the usual rolling hills of the plains, the shadows of taller bluffs and flat-top mesas showing against the star-lit sky. Sean tried to put himself into the minds of the raiders, relieved when he saw the tracks no longer dug in the dirt, which told him they had dropped back to a walk. He thought they would believe he could not follow them, since he was without a horse. And one man against their number would not fill them with fear. He hoped they would soon stop for the night, finding a campsite with water and cover.

He snapped his fingers to Indy, dropped to a walk, and waited for the wolf to come back to his side. When Indy approached, Sean stopped, putting his hands on his knees and breathing deep. He whispered to the wolf, "Gotta stop, boy. Don't wanna run up on 'em when I'm too tired to fight. Let's sit down here," motioning to the embankment of a low bluff, "and catch our breath."

———

UUWATCHIILAPISH, Iron Bull, was the leader of the war party that pursued the Lakota that had raided their village and stole their horses. But when the Lakota out-distanced them, he decided to turn back to their village. The men were sullen and angry at his decision, but when they saw the thin whisper of smoke beyond the bluff, it was Iron Bull that decided to take the prizes of three horses and the woman; at least they would not return empty-handed to their village. Taking the camp by surprise, the woman was easily captured but with only three horses, and two saddles, Bull knew there was only one man with the woman. Taking everything and tying the woman to her horse, they were soon back on the trail to their village.

At the insistence of Apitisée, Big Crane, Iron Bull had agreed to make camp for the night. Crane argued, "He is a white man, he will not follow! They are too lazy and weak. If he does, what can he do with so many of us?"

"We will camp there," Bull motioned to a bluff near a shallow creek bed. "No one is to touch the woman! She is my prize!" he ordered, knowing the others considered her fair game for all.

"She is the prize of all!" argued Crane.

Before Crane knew what happened, Iron Bull held the tip of his knife at his throat, "She is my prize!"

Crane held up an empty hand, showing no argument. When Bull removed the knife, Crane ordered the others,

"Leave the woman. She is Iron Bull's prize!" There was some grumbling, but the reputation of Iron Bull as a merciless warrior and leader stifled the group.

When camp was made, horses picketed, and bedrolls laid out, Bull directed Fox to start the fire and cook some of the meat from the fresh-killed deer. She soon had long strips hanging from several willow withes and dripping the juices into the fire. Although she didn't understand the words of the Crow, Bull made his orders known with sign language and his demeanor. She also noticed the leers and remarks that had been regularly given as they rode after he capture, had now ceased. The men kept their distance and seldom even looked at her, all except Bull. He stood behind her with his hand on her shoulder as she cooked, but that was the only time he touched her.

Fox was worried about Bear Chaser and she believed he would follow them, even though he was afoot. She was afraid he might try to take her from the Crow, and she wondered how she could keep him away so he would not be killed. Surely, he could not take her from so many, but she had a feeling deep within that he would somehow rescue her. She smiled at the thought and wondered how she could help. She would have to think it out, consider what he might do, and be ready. Maybe Indy would save her again! She thought of the big black wolf coming out of the darkness like he did before, only this time he would sink his teeth into this wretched Crow that had his hand on her shoulder.

———

SEAN LOOKED to the side at the bluff that rose from the

flats and started up the long slope. Although he didn't have his scope, and the light was dim, he hoped the captors had stopped and built a fire for their camp. If so, on a clear night like tonight, a flame could be seen for two to five miles. He squatted on his haunches and searched the darkness, hoping for at least a pinprick of light, anywhere. But there was none to be seen. He scanned again, unconsciously squinting, searching the entire horizon to the north and west, nothing.

With a simple wave, Indy started on the trail again, Sean following at the same pace. His legs were beginning to burn, his stomach taut, his neck tense, but he did not slow. Indy stayed to the middle of the wide trail of hoof-prints, and Sean knew the recent passage of horses ensured fewer obstacles like the big patches of prickly pear cactus usually found in these flats and not easily seen in the darkness. He caught his wind, breathed deeper, and stretched his stride, anxious to overtake the abductors. After another couple of miles, he slowed, brought Indy back and the two trudged up atop another low butte. With a deep breath, he sat down, and began his search. He could barely make out the black line that separated the horizon from the night sky, but the light from the wide band, called the Milky Way by whites and the Road Beyond by natives, delineated the darkness.

As he searched for the bright flame of a cookfire, he was disappointed again. He looked down to Indy, rubbed his neck and behind his ears, "Nothin' yet, boy. They must not a' been hungry!" He lifted his eyes for another search, moving from the west to the north and north-east, but there was no light. As he started to rise, something nagged at his consciousness, something wasn't right. He looked again, slowly, carefully, thoroughly. There! It wasn't the light of a fire, but a glow, showing against the bluff. He grinned, it was the glimmering of a fire below the ridge of a draw. "There they are boy. We got 'em now!"

He rose and the two took to the trail with renewed enthusiasm and optimism. But he was mindful as they trotted toward their target. Calculating all the while, he began to plot his attack, and attack he would, but first he had to know what he faced. He would have to wait, scout the camp after they ate and turned in for the night. Then he could approach and decide what to do, knowing he had little choice if Fox was to survive.

Although it was a quiet night, there was still a slight breeze that kicked up, intermittently forcing Sean to swing wide of the Crow camp, to approach downwind. Indy was a great ally, but the smell of a wolf would alarm the horses. When he bellied down beside the wolf, Sean watched as the fire died out and the men took to their blankets. He counted ten warriors, with one seated near the picket line to watch over the mounts. The others were scattered about, with one man next to Fox. Sean had seen by the dwindling light, Fox had been bound hand and foot, and the length of braided rawhide was kept in the hands of her captor. Sean continued to search the camp and the surrounding area as he contemplated his tactics. He would wait.

CHAPTER NINETEEN
FIGHT

THE PICKET LINE WAS STRETCHED FROM A GNARLED CEDAR to a rock pile at the edge of the bluff. Sean's horses were together at the end by the cedar and the look-out was seated near the tree. Knowing his horses would not be spooked by his smell, he crawled slowly toward the cedar, keeping in line behind the tree and out of the line of sight from the guard. He had ordered Indy to stay and the wolf obeyed, but his movement showed his desire to be with Sean. It took more than a quarter hour for Sean to reach the tree, and he silently moved closer to the guard. The man's chin was on his chest and he breathed evenly, telling Sean he was asleep. With his Bowie knife in hand, he made a stealthy step behind the man, and in one swift movement, put one hand over the guard's mouth and brought the razor-sharp blade across his throat. The lookout grabbed at Sean's wrist, made one frantic kick and slumped in death. Sean took the man's knife from his belt, put it in his and turned away.

He looked at the sleeping warriors, then the horses,

nothing moved. Dusty and the grey were watching Sean with interest but made no noise. Horses are social animals and tend to follow the lead of others. When the three horses at the end of the line showed no alarm, the others made no other move. He was glad to see his horses still had all their gear on, though the cinches were loosened, probably in anticipation of an early start in the morning. Most of the Indian ponies had some gear, though many of the warriors used the same blanket for sleeping as they used for their riding pad. Sean made his way along the picket line, cutting the leads of all the horses and letting them drop. All the animals stood where they were, most not knowing they were no longer tethered.

Sean dropped to a crouch and stealthily made his way back to Indy, leading their three horses. He ground tied Dusty, and with the leads of the other two dallied around the horn of his saddle, he knew the horses would stay. With a simple wave, the wolf came to his side and the two started for the other side of the camp. Most of the warriors, though scattered out and none close by another, were further back in the draw, away from the picket line and Fox and her captor were to the side, away from the others. Although his first thought was to take the warriors farthest back, he decided to free the woman first.

Even his father had said Sean was better at stealthily moving through the woods and Sean carefully chose every step as he moved at a low crouch toward the still form of Fox. As he neared, she moved slightly, but he wasn't surprised to see her eyes wide open watching his every move. She looked to Iron Bull, watched his chest rise and fall evenly, and looked back to Sean. With one slow move, he held the tether, cut it through, and handed the guard's knife to Fox. One step more and he was near the war leader. As he stepped to the side, the man's eyes flared open, but Sean's hand covered his mouth as he plunged the long blade of the Bowie into his chest, moving the blade side to side as the man struggled, kicking and thrashing, then dropped his arms and lay dead.

Fox was cutting her bonds and Sean looked at the others, but no one stirred. She put her hand to the neck of Indy, and as Sean watched the camp, Fox and the wolf circled around to the horses, followed closely by Sean. When they neared the animals. Sean snatched up his bow, nocked an arrow and watched the sleeping Crow. He whispered, "Tighten the cinches, check the packs. I already saw the rifles in the scabbards, so I don't think we're missing any . . ." He suddenly stepped into his bow, brought it to full draw and loosed the arrow. One of the warriors had risen, probably to relieve himself, and was approaching the body of their leader. The arrow caught the man in the neck and drove him to the ground with nothing more than a choking gurgle. Sean instantly nocked another arrow, whispered over his shoulder to Fox, "Ready?"

"Almost!" she answered in a whisper.

Sean searched the camp for movement, started to turn just as another man sat up and looked around. When the man threw the blankets aside, obviously alarmed, and stood, another arrow found its mark. The warrior staggered back, looked down at his chest to see only the fletching of the arrow protruding, lifted his eyes to the shadowy figure near some horses, and his knees gave way as he fell on his face. Again, Sean nocked an arrow, but

Fox spoke softly, "Let's go!" She had mounted and held the rein for Sean. With one last look at the camp, he swung aboard, and they started away from the Crow camp, keeping the horses at a walk. Sean twisted around in his saddle to watch behind them, as he held the bow across his pommel. He couldn't unstring it while he was mounted, and he wanted to be further away before they stopped.

When he judged they were about a mile and a half from the camp, he reined up, dropped down and unstrung the bow. He slipped the longbow into its sheath and hung the quiver from the tie-down behind the cantle and stepped back aboard. With a nod to Fox, they kicked the horses to a canter and made short work of leaving the country of the Crow.

The waning moon hung over his right shoulder and the multitude of stars shone as if they were trying to out-do one another for brilliance. Even the Milky Way seemed brighter as they wound their way through the maze of gullies, dry washes, and rolling hills. But both were almost giddy with relief and happiness. The moment that both doubted would come, was upon them. They were once again together and riding side-by-side in the lonesome but blessed darkness of the plains. Sean reached out and took Fox's hand in his, "It sure is good to see you sittin' pretty on that paint pony. For a while there, I wasn't sure if I'd ever see you again."

She smiled, her white teeth showing in the dim moon-light, "I was afraid you would come, and I was afraid you would not come."

Sean chuckled, "That's what boyfriends do!"

The laughter of Fox gave a special joy to Sean's heart

and even Indy seemed happy to hear her giggle and laugh as they rode in the dim light of early morning.

ALTHOUGH BOTH WERE RELIEVED at their escape, neither wanted to take any chance of being overtaken by vengeful Crow, and they pushed on through the night. When the rising sun chased the moon and stars from the sky, they stopped by a small creek for a short time of rest for the horses. Sean stripped them, let them roll and brushed them down with clumps of grass. After allowing the animals to water and graze for a while, they again took to the trail.

The horses ate as they walked, snatching bits of grass between strides and munching as they moved. With short stops for rest for both man and beast, by nightfall they had the North Platte in sight. They pushed on and made camp in a cluster of cottonwoods and dropped, exhausted, into their blankets. The rattle of trace chains brought Sean instantly awake and a quick glance showed a long line of whitetopped wagons moving on the trail on the far side of the river. He was standing with his pistol in hand when a rider stopped and hollered across, "Sleepin' in a little late, ain'tcha?"

Sean waved at the man, watched as he reined his mount around to catch up with the wagons, then turned to see Fox rising from her blankets. They smiled at one another, Sean with a bit of embarrassment showing as he realized he had slept so soundly and so late, but even Indy had been willing to snooze a little longer than usual. The horses were contentedly grazing in some deep grass by the river bank, and Fox stood, stretched, and asked, "Coffee?"

"Sure, I'd like some."

"No, I was asking if it was ready!" grinned Fox, looking at a speechless Sean.

CHAPTER TWENTY
LARAMIE

THE SUN WAS WELL UP WHEN SEAN AND FOX STARTED ON the trail back to Fort Laramie. It was quite a change to be traveling in the full light of day. Not only was it unusual to see the scenery, but even the sounds and smells were different. The cool of night carried sounds and somehow made them clearer and more distinct. The dust of the day moved with the slightest hint of a breeze, carrying the scents of the prairie with it. Those that are used to depending on all their senses for survival could easily identify the stench of decaying flesh from some dead creature. But the more subtle scents of deer, coyote, prairie dog, and others were borne on the tell-tale breezes of the flats.

It was a pleasant day and Fox turned her face to the sun, eyes closed, smiling, "I am happy!"

Sean grinned as he looked at her, smiling into the bright sunlight, "And what makes you so happy on this day?"

"It is a pretty day! And we are going to see my family!"

"Uh, we're still a few days away from the Fort."

"Yes, but you are going to get us some fresh meat, I will find some plants, and we will have a good meal when we camp! I am happy!"

Sean couldn't help but chuckle and grin at the giddiness of the woman, it was a good day and the warm sun made it even better. He leaned forward on the pommel, looking around, enjoying the arid landscape. A rocky bluff rose on his left, rimrock at the edge like a dusty crown, wind whipped pillars of sandstone resembled a scepter of the buried king. Below the bluff, the slope fell away to the myriad of mounds of a prairie dog town with the furry, fat rodents standing on their back legs, front legs dangling at their chests, as they watched the horses pass. The shadow of a winged predator crossed their path and the whistle pigs sounded the alarm then everyone ducked into their burrows to await the all-clear signal.

A large, flat, lichen-covered boulder sat lonely and forsaken, but a pair of lizards were contentedly sunning themselves, oblivious to any danger. Lizard wasn't on the Osprey's menu and they were too quick for any other predator, for now. A patch of white daisies stretched toward the river, and a smaller patch of paintbrush scattered drops of reddish-orange beside the trail. A broad spread of deep blue flowers with grass like petals caught Fox's attention, and she kicked her paint to a trot towards them. Sean looked, curiously, but followed.

She slipped from her saddle and ran into the flowers, clapping her hands excitedly. Sean sat watching, wondering, as Fox began to pull several of the plants up, and pluck the bulbous roots. When both hands were full, she looked up to Sean, "Bring me something to put these in!" she demanded, looking around at all the flowers, grinning.

Sean retrieved an empty flour sack from one of the panniers, walked to her side, "So, what has you so excited?"

"These are Chamas, or Camas, they are very good! I will cook them with our deer steak, and you will want more!"

"Hmmm, well if they're that good, why haven't I had them before?"

Fox stashed her trove in the pannier, mounted up, and started off with Sean in pursuit, somewhat surprised at her quick getaway. "So, now that you've got your roots, are you in a hurry to get to camp?"

She twisted around in her saddle, grinning over her shoulder at Sean, "Yes. I can taste them already! But, come up here," she motioned beside her, "there's something I want to ask you."

"Well, it'll hafta wait, we're crossing the river." He motioned to the wide part of the shallow river lacking ripples and promising a easy crossing. "That looks like the best spot I've seen, that gravel there and that bit of an island yonder, shows shallow water, so, with the main part of the trail over there, let's make it while the sun's high." He led the way and nudged Dusty into the murky water. It had often been said the North Platte was too thick to drink and too thin to plow, but with most of the spring runoff past, the water was cloudy but offered enough visibility to see the pebbly bottom.

Once across, they dropped to the ground, letting their horses have their usual shake to rid themselves of the excess water, although the water only once reached their bellies. They led the horses up the bank and once atop, Fox handed Sean the lead to her horse and ran back to retrieve another bag from the pannier. She trotted down the bank to some low growing bushes and ground-hugging greenery and started picking some early season strawberries and raspberries. In just a few moments, she returned, stashed her bag, and mounted up. Sean hurried and stepped into his stirrup to swing aboard Dusty to catch up with Fox.

"Hey! Hold on there! You said you had something you wanted to talk about, what was it?"

She nodded her head, reined up until he could come alongside, then asked, "What does your God say about you killing those Crow warriors?" She had a sober expression and cocked her head to the side, waiting for an answer.

They started off together as Sean began, "Uh, well, first off, He says *Thou shalt not kill.* Now, a lot o' folks get that wrong, 'cause there's lotsa times in the Bible that God's people had to kill others, like David and Goliath."

"Who?"

"Oh, that's another story I'll tell ya' sometime. But there's times when men have to kill, like in a war and stuff, but it's like the elders and chiefs of the Miniconjou said about always doin' what's right. That's what my pa always said, 'Son, no matter what, you've got to do what's right.' Now, I didn't kill those Crow just because they were Crow or because I wanted to kill somebody, I did it 'cause the right thing to do was to save you from them, and that's what I had to do to get you away from them. Now, you tell me, was that the right thing to do?"

"Yes. It makes me happy that you did the right thing."

"See, I've already had a little talk with God about that. I asked Him to forgive me for havin' to kill 'em, and I sure enough don't feel bad about it."

"Does your God always forgive you?"

"Yes. And the good part is, it's not because of us, but because He's a God of grace."

Fox looked at him, forehead wrinkled, showing her lack of understanding, and Sean answered, "It's because He's good, even if we're not."

She nodded her head, smiling. "It is that way with *Wakan Tanka* but our prayers are carried by the smoke from the sacred pipe."

"Do you remember any of the beliefs of your family in Sante Fe?" asked Sean.

"No, I was young when I was taken. I remember my mother and father, but that is all." She looked to Sean, "With the whites, what does a man do to take a woman to his lodge?"

Sean turned just a little to look at Fox's expression, then answered, "You mean like husband and wife?"

"Is that what you call it when a man and a woman are joined?"

"Uh, yeah, it's called getting married. You see the man asks the woman, well usually, and then he gets her father's permission, and then they have a wedding by a preacher or missionary or something like that."

"Oh, that is like our people. But sometimes the father chooses the man, but other times it is just the man and woman. With our people, after the rite of *Awicalowanpi,* a woman must be pure and cannot look at a man, unless they are to be together. And she cannot be alone with a man until they have been joined. If she is found to be with a man in any way, she would no longer be good to be joined."

"Uh, hold on. Didn't your father, Crow Dog, send you to go with me to the other camps?"

"No, I told him. But he knew you could be killed if you did not have one of the people with you, so he did not keep me from going."

"So, now that you've been with me, alone, all this time. Does that mean you could not be joined with a warrior of your people?"

"Only with you, boyfriend," she said, lifting her head proudly.

IT WAS two additional days of traveling before they sighted Fort Laramie. A long two days of pensive thought by Sean, trying to comprehend all that Fox had said about her people's traditions and 'joining' or marriage. Maybe this 'boyfriend' thing had gone too far, but what could he do about it now? Nothing had happened between them, although he had to admit he was quite fond of the woman. He had become very accustomed and comfortable with her presence, and she was the first thing he wanted to see every morning, but marriage? As he thought about it, he couldn't see himself married like his Pa and Ma were, having their own cabin and all. But he couldn't imagine himself without Fox by his side, either. Whenever he thought about her, he found himself smiling and thinking about their time together. He even imagined what it would be like to be married and to always be together and that made him smile even more. Then he thought of the many stories his folks shared about their early years together and pictured him and Fox traveling the mountains, making friends, building a home. He breathed deep, smiling, thinking those were mighty good thoughts.

When they first sighted Fort Laramie, both were amazed at the many tipis gathered all around the walls. Sean guessed there were well over a hundred, and it was evident the different bands were clustered together, but all were similar. He looked to Fox, "Can you tell which camp is your father's?"

They were on a slight knob of a hill overlooking the winding North Platte and the bluff that held the fort. The main gate was on the south side, but the different bands were arrayed on the north and west and some on the south away from the gate, with the river to the east.

"There!" She was standing in her stirrups and motioning to the west side of the fort. With a broad smile, it was evident she recognized the big lodge of her father by the painting and position of the lodge. As he thought about going to the lodge of her father, he remembered what Fox had said about the role of a father among the people.

She had explained that when a man wants a woman, he must offer gifts to the father. If the father accepts the gifts, then she can be joined to the man. If not, he must bring better gifts or accept his rejection.

"What kind of gifts?" he had asked.

"Horses, blankets, weapons, sometimes food, skins, other things."

"How much?"

"Whatever he believes the woman is worth!"

He thought of that now. His pa had left him a goodly amount of gold coin just in case he might need some money for supplies and other things. Maybe this was the 'other things' he mentioned.

CHAPTER TWENTY-ONE
WAGONS

IT WAS AN IMPRESSIVE SIGHT, THE LONG LINE OF DOUBLE-hooked, tall-sided, freight wagons with each pair pulled by the extended teams of ten mules, driven by the loud, sometimes vulgar, muleskinners that could crack a black-snake bullwhip with the sound of a rifle shot. The drivers deftly maneuvered the long snake of mule teams and wagons through the Indian camps to the front gate of Fort Laramie. The line stalled in place after the first two pairs entered the fort. The muleskinners set the wagon brakes, let the long lines droop on the backs of the mules, and climbed down from their lofty perch high atop the wagons.

Sean turned to Fox, "Let's find us a place down by the river. We'll make camp and then you can go to your family while I go report to the commandant."

"Will you not come to see my family?" asked Fox. She spoke quietly, looking down and fearful that he would leave her and not return.

"Yes, I'll come. But first I have to report to the soldier

chief. I am a scout and I must report in when I return. And I want to make sure the supplies in those wagons are for the people. And, we're out of coffee and I could sure use some, since you've taken a liking to it," he smiled at her and the relief showed on her face. He knew she had been afraid he would leave her, but he had pretty well decided he would have to talk to her father. The thought of being without her didn't appeal to him at all.

An undercut bank amidst a thick cluster of cotton-woods that sheltered a grassy flat at the edge of the river provided an exceptional campsite for Sean and Fox. Once the horses had been stripped, watered, rubbed down, and tethered, and the camp gear stacked, Sean swung the saddlebags over his shoulder. He said, "I'll finish what I need to do in the fort, then I'll come to your father's lodge. Just see if Crow Dog can keep Blue Eagle out of our way. I don't feel like getting into another fight with him or any other."

Fox giggled, "I think he will not be there. You made him look bad."

"That's the problem, he might want to try to get back at me." He looked down at Indy, "Are you taking him?" he nodded toward the wolf.

"My people know you as the man with the wolf, and they have told others about you. It will make me proud when you and Indy come to the village to our lodge," she lifted her head as she spoke, a slight grin showing.

Sean chuckled, "Alright then, c'mon boy, let's go get us some coffee!"

THEIR CAMP WAS DOWNRIVER from the fort, but an easy

walk to the gate. When Fox directed her steps straight toward the village, Sean turned to walk to the main gate, passing part of the long line of wagons as he did. The two pair of wagons and the teams of mules filled the central compound of the fort, and the muleskinners and their helpers were busy unloading the wagons. With each wagon carrying three to five tons of goods, it would be a while before all were emptied. Sean noticed most of the goods were blankets, trade goods, staples, and more. Sean walked to the commandant's office and entered to make his report.

Captain Steele stood and greeted him, "Sean Saint, welcome back! General Harney filled me in on your assignment. Have a seat, and let's catch up, shall we?"

"Captain," addressed Sean, extending his hand to shake with Steele. He sat down and to begin his report but was interrupted by Steele.

"Before I forget," he began as he slipped the lap drawer of the desk open and retrieved an envelope, "You've got a letter here. Must be from your family in St. Louis." He handed the envelope to Sean, who looked at the handwriting, smiled when he recognized it and answered, "Yessir. That's my mother's handwriting. She's in St. Louis seeing to my sister's education."

"That's fine, fine. Now, tell me what you found on your scout," he instructed.

Sean began sharing the details of his meeting with the Brulé, avoiding any mention of his set-to with Blue Eagle, and the good report from Crow Dog. He explained about seeing but not meeting with the Oglala, and their journey to the camp of the Miniconjou and his profitable meeting with the council and their decision to send a delegation to the fort for the supplies. The captain was concerned about the conflict between the Crow and the Oglala, and the Sioux pushing into the Crow territory.

"Well, Captain, that's been going on since before the treaty. The Sioux, none of 'em, the Brulé, Oglala, Miniconjou, or any of the others, agree with the territories of that treaty. Up north, the Sioux are pushing out the Assiniboine, the Arikara, Mandan, and others as well."

The captain leaned back in his chair, eyeing him, considering. "Sean, I don't know how much you know about the war back east, but there's a lot going on. The general told me before he left that they were putting together some volunteer regiment to come out here and take over. I think he said it's the Seventh Ohio, but it's a Lieutenant Colonel William Collins. Now, I've got some men here that have southern sympathies and they're looking for any excuse to just high-tail it and join the Confederacy. Now, you saw how many Indians are just outside the fort, and if they decide to take it, there's not a whole lot the few of us can do."

"Captain, those that I talked to aren't interested in anything but getting what's coming to them. Now, if those wagons out there have the full measure of commodities they were promised, I don't think you have anything to be concerned about."

"That's just it, Sean. Now that we've got a telegraph here, there was a message that came in for the leader of the teamsters. Not all those wagons are going to stay here at the fort. They're supposed to take them to the Colorado gold fields. Even if they had the full measure to start with, which I doubt, they're not planning on giving it out."

"What can we do to stop them?" asked Sean, growing concerned.

"I have no authority. My orders are to just keep the peace as the goods are distributed. Although the fort sutler is the one distributing, it's by order of the Commissioner of Indian Affairs, William Dole."

"You said you have a telegraph; can you send him word and make sure he tells his men to distribute the goods?"

"The telegraph was from him. He's the one telling them to take it to the gold fields!"

Sean stood, extended his hand, "Well, Captain. Sorry I didn't get to know you better, but you're gonna have about a thousand mad Indians coming down on you pretty soon."

The captain stood to shake Sean's hand, "I understand. Guess I'll have to figure out what to do, but it's not going to be to try to fight a thousand warriors with less than a hundred malcontents."

Sean walked from the commandant's office to the Sutler's store, Indy beside him. They entered the store, and were greeted by the Sutler, "Get that dog outta here!" he shouted. Indy let one lip curl up to show a long fang and a low growl as Sean answered, "You tell him. And don't insult him by calling him a dog, he don't like it. Most wolves don't!" At the mention of wolf, the sutler looked back to Indy, saw the animal preparing to pounce and stepped back, "Uh, uh, keep him back, please! I got work to do!"

With an open palm, Sean signaled Indy and the animal bellied down beside him. He asked the Sutler, "I need a good rifle. What'cha got?"

The Sutler smiled, anticipating a good sale, and pointed to a rack behind him, "I got Sharps, Hawkens, couple o' Kentucky flinters. What'cha interested in?"

"The Sharps. Let me have a look."

The Sutler took down a Sharps, opened the breech and handed it to Sean. Sean looked at the rifle, back at the trader, "Paper cartridge?"

"Yeah, but I got 'nother'n coming that uses brass cartridges."

"You got some paper cartridges here?"

"Yup, shore do."

When the trading and dickering was finished, Sean walked from the store carrying a sizable bundle over one arm and his saddle-bags loaded with coffee and sugar. The rest of the supplies could wait until the next day. He started from the Sutler's, arms full and stepped to the boardwalk in front, heading for the front gate, when he saw a familiar figure by the freight wagons. He stopped, put his bundle of goods down on the boardwalk, spoke to Indy, "Stay," and pointed to the bundle. The wolf bellied down beside it, laying his head across the blanket.

SEAN WALKED TOWARD THE FREIGHTER, certain this was the man they befriended when they scouted for the college boys from Yale. Bucky had been the head of the teamsters that brought them out from St. Louis and fought with him and his pa against the Sioux. He walked close and called out, "Bucky?"

A big burly whiskered man turned, scowling, looking ready to fight, and saw Sean and frowned. He squinted, stepped forward, "Sean? Sean Saint?"

Sean grinned, extended his hand and walked toward the big man. The bulbous belly shook as he laughed and slapped Sean's hand aside as he took the young man in a bear hug and lifted him off the ground, his deep laugh echoing throughout the fort. He sat Sean down, gave him a chance to catch his breath then asked, "Is your pa with you?"

"No, he had to guide the general and his men back to St. Louis."

The big man's countenance turned sad, and he shook his head. "Dad gum it! I was hopin' he'd be here. When's he gettin' back?"

"I dunno, but not anytime soon. What's wrong, you look upset?"

"There's trouble brewin' Sean, and I ain't sure what to do 'bout it." He looked around to see if anyone was near, cautious about what he said.

Sean looked around as well, then in a low voice, "We're camped downstream a short way, next to the river. I'll be there later, so, you come on down and have a meal with us and we'll talk about it. Savvy?"

The big man nodded, turned away and went back to unloading the big wagons. Sean retrieved his bundle and started away. As he walked from the fort, everyone stepped back from the big wolf and stared at the man with the beast beside him and his arms loaded. The people of the village of Crow Dog had much the same reaction, but many recognized Sean and the wolf and several gave friendly greetings. Some followed as he made his way to the center of the camp and stopped when he saw Crow Dog seated in front of his lodge.

As she helped her mother prepare the meal, Fox

paused, watching Sean come near, and smiled. She looked at the bundle and dropped her eyes, trying to keep from jumping with excitement. She watched as Sean stopped in front of Crow Dog, sat down the bundle and without saying anything, and began to unroll the package. He stretched out one blanket, took two Bowie knives with scabbards and lay them on the blanket. Two skinning knives were laid beside three bars of lead and three containers of powder. A bullet mold and a wiping stick were placed alongside the powder. Two more blankets, Hudson Bay five-points, were folded and placed beside the rest. Four boxes of paper cartridges were sat to one side, because he knew they would be unknown to the chief.

Satisfied, Sean stood, unwrapped the last blanket from the Sharps rifle and with the rifle leaning against his hip, he made a big to-do of folding the last blanket to place atop the others. Then he lifted the rifle to his shoulder, sighted down the barrel, and laid the rifle on the blanket. He stepped back and with a sweep of his hand toward the blanket, said, "For the great Crow Dog."

Sean had casually watched the chief as each item was placed, saw his growing excitement and attempt to maintain his composure and dignity, and when the rifle was placed at the top of the blanket, farthest from the chief, he could contain himself no longer and quickly stood and made his way to reach for the rifle. The chief had never seen a Sharps but had heard of the big buffalo gun. His elation was obvious, but as he lifted the rifle to his shoulder, he frowned at the breech action, not knowing how it worked. He looked to Sean, waiting for an explanation. Sean stepped to the cartridge boxes, took out one and from the can of percussion caps, took one of the copper caps. He slowly and carefully loaded the rifle, showing the chief how it was done, closed the breech, placed the cap, and brought it to full cock with the rear set trigger. He explained, "This is the firing trigger. Very touchy." He looked up and pointed at the tip of an exceptionally tall tipi pole with a long ribbon flying and said, "Shoot at that."

The chief took a stance, lifted the rifle to his shoulder, aimed, and slowly squeezed the trigger. Fox had watched and told her mother to cover her ears as she did. When the big rifle roared, most of the villagers shouted in surprise and shock, and the chief was rocked back on his heels, but he came forward, smiling. He was pleased with the gifts, especially the rifle, which would have easily cost fifteen to twenty horses in any trade, but this was a gift like no other. He grinned at Sean, nodding his head in agreement at the prizes for his daughter. Sean looked to Fox and her mother, both of whom were smiling broadly and hugging each other. Sean smiled and went to his bride-to-be and the two embraced.

CHAPTER TWENTY-TWO
MULESKINNERS

FOX GLADLY SERVED UP THE LAST OF THE CAMAS BULBS with turnips, potatoes, and skunk cabbage. The juicy strips of deer steak hung over the edges of the tin plate and the fresh coffee was steaming as Bucky and Sean sat opposite one another, both on downed grey cottonwood logs. Bucky said, "Boy, it's sure'nuff good to see you. Why, you look like you've grown two feet since we brought them rich kids out on their buffalo hunt!" He leaned forward and spoke softly, "I thought you and that Frenchy's little girl was gonna be a pair, whatever happened to them?"

Sean chuckled, "Ah, they wanted to go back to their home in the north. Seems her mom had a man all picked out for her among the Santee Sioux, her people. We were just good friends, more like pals than anything else."

"Is this'n," nodding toward Fox, "your woman now?" asked Bucky.

"You could say that. I gave her father the bride price, or dowry, or whatever you wanna call it. Her ma's preparing for the big ceremony. So, yeah, she's gonna be my wife."

"Congratulations boy, I'm proud of you!" He looked from Sean to Fox, his face showing a sober expression, then he took the telegram from his pocket and handed it to Sean. After the address portion that showed the telegram was from Harris and Lafferty, owners of the warehouse, it read,

The six wagons top loaded with boxes marked 'tools' are to be driven to Denver City by way of Julesburg. Mr. Lafferty from the Quartermaster warehouse in Independence will join the wagons in Julesburg. He will be in charge of distributing the cargo in Denver City. The wagons will be loaded with ore for the return to Independence.

William P. Dole, Commissioner of Indian Affairs

Sean looked to Bucky, "What's in those wagons?"

"It ain't all tools, that's for sure! Those boxes are loaded with rifles, powder, and lead. The rest of the loads are some tools, but mostly staples; sugar, flour, salt, things that go for lots of money in mining camps."

"But all that was supposed to go to the Sioux!"

"Ummmhumm, and I don't think they're gonna like watchin' them wagons leave the fort still loaded."

"No, they're not. I have talked with some of the chiefs and promised I would do whatever I could to ensure they'd get what was promised." He looked to Bucky, "Are you supposed to go with the wagons goin' to Julesburg, or back to Independence?"

"That's my choice. I'm the head of the teamsters, and I've been the one in charge comin' outchere, but I have another fella, Charlie Canterbury, that'll take whatever bunch I don't."

"Can you trust him?" asked Sean.

"Well, he'll do what he's told, but he'll fight for them wagons no matter which ones he takes. What'chu thinkin'?"

"I don't rightly know yet, but if those Sioux don't get their annuities, it won't be safe for anybody; wagon train, pilgrim, trader, trapper, anybody."

"What're we gonna do?"

"First, I've got to have a sit-down with Old Chief Stone of the Oglala, then I'll talk to some of the others and decide. You try to take your time unloading the rest of the wagons, gimme a little time, if you can." He thought for a moment, looked to Bucky, "There's somethin' else that's naggin' at me. That war back east, 'course you know more about it than I do, but what's goin' on?"

"There's been a lotta talk, lotta fellas in the army an' such have split and taken off to the south, can't hardly talk about it without somebody wantin' to fight. After the attack on Sumpter, and all them states secedin', mostly it was a lotta talk, arguin' fightin' among the politicians."

"The last I heard, there were about a half-dozen states that were leavin', how many now?"

"I'm thinkin' the count was up to ten, with others ponderin'. Tennessee, Missouri, and Kentucky were thinkin' 'bout it. But I think Tennessee'll do it, but not too sure 'bout Missouri and Kentucky," explained Bucky.

"An' all them folks talkin' 'bout the savage red man. Don't sound to me like they're any smarter!"

"Have you heard anything from your pa? Didn't you say he went to St. Louis?" asked Bucky, remembering his time with Tate and the way they prayed together. His life had been changed considerably since that time and he believed he had Tate to thank for it.

Sean grinned, patted his pocket, and said, "That reminds me, I got a letter from Ma." He dug out the envelope and carefully opened it, unfolded the paper and began to read.

Dearest Sean,

We hope this letter finds you well and happy. Your father had a good trip with the General and enjoyed the time with the soldiers. Although they met up with some of the Jayhawkers in Kansas, it went without incident. He has been here at the Inn and we have enjoyed our time together.

The conflict between the states has most in Missouri concerned about the future. General Harney was in command of the St. Louis Arsenal, but an underling, Captain Lyon, took control and met a force of secessionists under the governor who tried to take St. Louis for the Confederacy. Several days of rioting and fighting resulted in many deaths of both soldiers and civilians, but hopefully, all that is over, and we now have peace.

However, an old friend of your father's, Colonel Kit Carson, has asked your father to join him as a scout for the New Mexico Volunteers. Colonel Canby believes Confederate General Sibley will come from Texas and try to take New Mexico and move on to Colorado and the west. Carson believes your father will be of great help since he knows the area well. Although it has not been decided, I see the restlessness in your father and believe he will join Carson.

Sadie is doing well in school, but we both miss you. Please be careful in all that you do and let us know about everything.

Your loving mother and father, and sister,

Maggie, Tate, and Sadie.

He sat quiet for a moment, looking at the letter and thinking about his family. Fox had seated herself on the log next to him and put her arm through the crook of his elbow, resting her cheek on his shoulder. "I would like to meet your family."

Sean smiled, looked to her uplifted eyes, "You will, you will. And they will love you!"

Bucky moved to put a stick in the fire, "Sounds like your pa's gonna be gettin' in the fight!"

"Yeah, he has been friends with Carson since he first came west. That man took my father under his wing and showed him all about the mountains. And to hear Pa tell it, it was Carson that got him to take Ma on the search for her father and of course, they ended up married. He also said he and Carson married their first wives from the same tribe of the Arapaho. They were friends or something."

Fox looked to Sean, "Your mother was Arapaho?"

He chuckled, "No, that was before my time. Pa's first wife, who died, was an Arapaho."

"Oh," answered Fox, leaning against her man again.

Sean looked back to Bucky, "I think I'm gonna hafta figger somethin' out about those wagons. Cuz if the Sioux don't get what they're supposed to, the war out here's gonna make the one back east look like kids stompin' in a mud puddle!" He breathed heavy, looked around, and added, "I need to meet with the Oglala, try to see what they're thinkin' or plannin' and then see what can be done to keep those wagons from goin' to the goldfields." He looked to Bucky, "When do you think those wagons'll be leavin'? And who's gonna be takin' em?

"If you mean the ones for the goldfield, those fellas

will hafta help the rest of 'em to finish unloadin' the other wagons. That'll take all day tomorrow, then they'll probably leave the next morning. And since I know what they're doin' and not knowin' what you're gonna do, I think I'll let Charlie take 'em. I don't think yore pa would like it if I got in a shootin' fight with his son!"

"I don't think I'd like it much either!" answered Sean, grinning at the big man.

CHAPTER TWENTY-THREE
OGLALA

SEAN AND FOX, WITH INDY BETWEEN THEM, WALKED INTO the camp of the Oglala. It was not unusual for white men to come into their camp while they were at Fort Laramie, but the presence of the black wolf demanded everyone's attention. They walked to the central compound and to the large lodge of the chief. Commonly, the chief's lodge was the largest and most prominent in the camp, not just because it was the chief's, but it was used for the gathering of the council and must be large enough to accommodate the large number. Often twenty feet and more in diameter, it was the largest of the camp. Although the leadership of this village of the Oglala was soon to pass from Old Chief Stone to *Wašíčuŋ Ťhašúŋke* or He-Has-A-White-Man's-Horse, this lodge was that of Chief Stone.

An older warrior stepped before them as they neared the lodge and stopped them with his hand held before them. "I am Lone Man. Why do you come to the lodge of our chief?"

"I am Bear Chaser, this is my woman, White Fox,

daughter of Crow Dog of the Brulé. I have come to talk to your chief about the supplies and the treaty." He reached to his belt and brought out a sheathed Bowie knife, "This is a gift for your chief."

Lone Man had stayed to the side of Sean, keeping him between the wolf and himself. Hesitating to take his eyes off the wolf, he glanced down at the knife, recognizing it as a special gift and took it from Sean. "You stay, I will speak to our chief." He turned and scratched at the side of the entry flap of the chief's lodge. At a word from inside the tipi, he lifted the flap back and entered, dropping the flap behind him to signal to others not to enter.

As they waited, Fox said, "That is Lone Man, he is a Brulé, but his son is *Maȟpíya Lúta*, Red Cloud, he married an Oglala, Pretty Owl, and he is a great warrior and leader among the Oglala. It is said he will one day be a chief of his own village."

Lone Man came from the lodge, motioned for a young man to come and spoke directions to him, sending him on his way. The old warrior looked to Sean and Fox, nodded for them to come forward. Sean signaled for Indy to lay and stay, then started toward the lodge. When they neared, he held the flap back, and they entered. The old chief waved his hand for them to be seated across the fire. When he looked at Fox, he said, "You are the child of Crow Dog," and appeared to wait for her to answer.

Fox nodded respectfully, "Yes my chief, I am White Fox. My father is Crow Dog. This is Bear Chaser of the Arapaho. He is the son of Longbow."

The mention of the name of Longbow brought a light of recognition to the chief's eyes as he turned to look at Sean.

"I am told you want to speak of the supplies and the treaty," he said, again in a tone that was as much a question as a statement.

"Yes, Chief Stone, I would like . . ." but the upheld hand of the chief stopped him.

"We will wait for the others." He reached for a pipe that lay at his side, checked the bowl for tobacco, tamped down what was there, and reached for a twig at the fire to light the pipe. Once it was lit, he lifted it to the four directions, up to father sky and down to mother earth, took a long draft, exhaled the smoke, and passed the pipe to Sean.

Sean accepted the pipe, looked to Fox who spoke with her eyes for him to copy the chief. Sean lifted the pipe to the four directions, up to the sky and down to the earth, put it to his lips and drew in a deep draught, stifled a cough, and exhaled the smoke, before returning the pipe to the chief.

As the chief sat the pipe aside, several others started filing into the lodge, seating themselves near the chief, all facing Sean and Fox. Once the others were seated, Chief Stone motioned for Sean to stand and speak.

As he rose, Fox whispered, "Say your name first."

He nodded to her, and looked around the group before he began, "I am Bear Chaser, son of Longbow. We have lived with the Arapaho, Ute, and Comanche, but are friends to all. I am a scout for the soldier fort, I was asked by General Harney, who you call Butcher, to learn about the great Lakota people and to help bring peace to the plains." He paused and watched the others as they listened, showing no reaction.

"I have spoken to Crow Dog of the Brulé, One Horn of

the Miniconjou, and now to the great Oglala. The other Lakota have told me they have been lied to by the whites. What was promised in the treaty of Horse Creek has not been given. I agree with you that is wrong. I promised the other leaders that I would do what I can for you to get all that was promised."

The chief motioned for him to be seated, and Sean dropped down beside Fox. He looked to the chief as the man spoke, "We have heard of the white man that has a black wolf as a friend and rides with a Lakota woman." He looked to Fox, "Are you his woman?"

Fox lifted her head, chin high, and spoke boldly, "This man has paid my father the bride price, and we will be joined soon."

Several of those around the edge of the tipi, smiled, and nudged one another. The chief also smiled and looked back to Sean. "You watched us pass from the Old Woman Hills but did not come to our village to speak. You went to the Miniconjou. Now you speak of supplies that are already here. What can you do to make that different?"

"Because of the war among the white men in the east, supplies are threatened, and there are those that don't want to send supplies to the Sioux, but to keep them for their warriors in the east."

"We have heard of this war. Are all white men fighting?"

"There are many that are fighting, but not all."

Stone looked to the others, "Maybe they will kill each other, and we will not have to fight them!" His comment was received with much enthusiasm and chatter, many beating on the ground with their tomahawks and fists as they shouted in agreement.

Sean dropped his head, trying to keep a sober expression, but chuckling inside at the possibility, thinking that would be one solution. He continued, "I have learned of the possibility that not all these supplies will be given to your people, but some would be taken to the whites to the south."

That remark was met with anger and shouting, some insisting that all whites are liars. Sean did his best to ignore their response. "I ask that you give me time to find out if this is true and to do what I can to stop it."

Stone looked at him, and at the others, waiting for anyone to speak. One man raised his fist, "I am called Spider. What can you, one man, do to stop the soldiers from taking the supplies?"

"Spider, I do not know for sure that those that have the supplies will try to take them, but if they do, and if I need help, I will come to the Lakota for warriors to keep this from happening."

Another man spoke, "I am Standing Elk, chief of the Oglala. Why should we believe that you would go against your own people to get the supplies for the Lakota?"

"I would not go against my own people. But I will do what is right. If there are those that would lie and steal, no matter if they are white, Lakota, or any other people, I will go against those that do wrong. All I ask is that you give me time to find those that do wrong. I do not wish any man, white or Lakota, to die and if I can fix this without any killing, then that is what I will do."

Another stood and turned a fierce countenance toward Sean, "I am Spotted Eagle. I do not believe this white man. He lies like all white men! He wants to take the supplies without killing because he is afraid to die! Let me kill him now before the supplies are taken and then we will kill all the whites who would steal from us!" He spat the words hatefully, and others shouted their agreement.

Fox jumped to her feet, "I am a warrior among our people! This man fought Blue Eagle and defeated him but spared his life! His wolf saved me from an attack by other wolves, and when the Crow took me, he crept into their camp of ten warriors, killed four of them and took me back! He is more of a warrior than this man Spotted Eagle! If he," nodding toward her man, "would allow it. I could take this man of wind and words and kill him myself!" she shouted at the crowd, angrily pointing at Spotted Eagle.

Sean had stood when she started her rampage and waited until she was finished, slipped his arm around her waist and addressed the crowd calmly. "If it is the will of this council, I will meet Spotted Eagle, and we will fight. But my fight is not with the Lakota. It is with those that do wrong. Will this council give your decision?"

CHAPTER TWENTY-FOUR
CONFAB

They walked together, Indy at their side, as they left the camp of the Oglala. They were pensive as they walked, looking at the villagers around them, knowing these were people that had come to rely on the supplies from the white man. Sean looked down at Fox, "Do you think they'll give us much time?"

The decision of the council was to allow Sean time to resolve the possible theft of the supplies before they took any action. But the amount of time was not determined. Now that they knew the usual excuses and lies would probably be given, Sean knew they would react quickly and with no regard for the lives of any of the white men.

"The decision of the council was given in a way that did not bind the warriors. Any of the war leaders, Standing Elk, Red Cloud, Horse, who is called Spider, or Spotted Eagle, could get up a war party and attack the wagons or soldiers."

Sean started to respond but was stopped when his

name was called from behind. He turned to see a man approaching, attired in the usual beaded-buckskin leggings and tunic of the Lakota, but his hair was brown and grey, and his complexion was tanned. Sean immediately recognized him as a white man and paused to wait.

"Bear Chaser," began the man as he extended his hand to shake, the typical white man's greeting, "I am Thomas Twiss, I am the agent for the Oglala."

"Mr. Twiss, it is good to meet you, but I was told you had been removed as agent, is that right?" asked Sean.

The man dropped his head, and answered, "Yes, that is true. But I have connections in Washington trying to appeal that decision."

Sean looked the man over, and responded, "I almost didn't recognize you as a white man."

"Let us walk as we talk, please," he asked, motioning to the path between the tipis toward the fort. "I have lived with the Oglala for some time now, I too took a woman of the Sioux as my wife," nodding toward Fox, 'her name is Mary, she is the daughter of Standing Elk, the man you met in the council."

"General Harney tol' me 'bout you living with the Oglala, but he also said Lincoln removed you from the position as agent. There were some accusations you had been skimming off the top and selling the supplies to some traders, is that true?"

"Well, yes, sort of, you see, what we were doing was selling some of the things the people didn't need and trading them for the powder and lead that had been promised but not delivered. The people have become pretty dependent on using rifles for hunting. It's a lot easier to bring down a buffalo with a rifle than a lance. And there's a few other things you need to know before you go any further with this."

As they walked to Sean and Fox's camp by the river, Twiss explained about the many problems the Sioux and the other tribes had since the signing of the treaty in '51. "The men that put that treaty together didn't bother to get all the history from the different tribes. For instance, the traditional lands of the Lakota were split and much of it assigned to the Crow. The Kiowa, Comanche, Apache, all refused to be a part of the signing because the white man was trying to use things like rivers and mountain ranges as natural barriers and territory lines without regard to the sacred lands and traditional lands of the different peoples."

Twiss continued explaining the history of the conflicts since the signing of the treaty. He spoke of the Grattan Massacre and the events that followed, including the Battle of Blue Water Creek or Ash Hollow when General Harney had attacked a village with cannon and soldiers, killing eighty-six, men, women, and children, and taking seventy more captive. He went on to explain about Harney's demands to turn over some warriors that had attacked a mail wagon and how he, Twiss, had sent the men to Fort Leavenworth, but later wrote to President Franklin Pierce and told both sides of the account, which resulted in the warriors being pardoned and released.

"Harney was given the name 'Mad Bear' after that. But he still wanted to wipe out all the Lakota. He had removed me as agent, but the Interior Department restored me." He chuckled at a memory, "It was after that when I met my wife, and we started a family." He smiled and continued, "I put together a plan for a treaty after I talked with the Lakotas, Cheyenne, and Arapaho. All agreed to settle in certain areas, learn to farm and all, and all agreed and signed. But Congress rejected it without giving it a decent chance to work!"

They came to the camp and Sean motioned for Twiss to be seated, and Fox took the coffee-pot to get some fresh water and brew a pot. Twiss picked up a stone and chucked it at the river, "That was just last year. Since then, I've lived with the Oglala and have been accepted by them as a part of their village." He chuckled again, "We have two daughters and one son. My son is just over a year old and growing mighty fast."

"Do you miss living with your family, the one back east, I mean?"

"I'm happy here. These are good people. I have found the villagers to be loving, helpful, and more honest and forthright than any community I lived in before coming west. Oh, sure, there's some things that I miss, and I would like to see my family again, but I have a good life here. And I will continue to work for these people, even though I have no official capacity."

"But I'm sure you wanted to talk about more than the history of the people and the treaty," stated Sean, waiting for more.

"Yes, but I wanted you to understand these people so you could understand whatever they do. You see, they have been lied to and cheated so many times, they have no reason to believe anything any white man says. Within days after they signed the treaty of Horse Creek, the soldiers were allowing white settlers onto the lands of the Lakota. The wagon trains were supposed to stay on the Oregon Trail and didn't, and more. But here's what you need to know. I know my wife's father, Standing Elk, and Red Cloud. They are already recruiting warriors for what they expect will happen. Now that they know the freighters might try to get away with some of the wagons; they are ready to stop them."

"What about the council giving me time to stop them or prevent it?"

"Oh, they will wait, but not so long as to allow the wagons to get away," explained Twiss. "Those supplies mean everything to the people, especially the rifles, powder, and lead. They won't let those be taken from them again. They know that with the war in the east, there might not be another shipment of goods, and these wagons are loaded for them. So . . ." he shrugged his shoulders to emphasize his point.

Fox joined in, "That is the way the people of my village feel also. My mother said many have talked about taking everything from the soldier fort, and from the fort downstream, the one you call Fort Bernard."

"If one band starts it, all will join in, and there won't be anything left of either Laramie or Bernard. The people are that angry," explained Twiss.

"Is there anything you can do to stop them?" asked Sean, hopefully.

"Why? I agree with them. If they go hungry, my lodge will also be hungry. The people know of the war in the east, and the elders have said that for the people to rely on the handouts of the whites is wrong. They have even said that the one that takes handouts is no longer a man."

"Can't say as I disagree with 'em, but it still boils down to a whole lot o' people gettin' killed."

"It is the way of the white man," started Twiss but was interrupted by Sean.

"Hold on there, you're a white man, and you're talkin' as if you're an Indian!"

Twiss dropped his head, clasped his hands together as he took a deep breath, "If I am forced to choose between the Lakota and the white man, it would be a hard choice, but I think I'd hafta choose the Lakota." He paused, moved on his seat to find a more comfortable position, "The way the politicians and others have done, is to make the Indian dependent on his gifts and tools, pots, blankets, rifles, and more. Then they take it away and demand more land for the settlers, make a treaty, and refuse to live up to it. Then they want more land, fewer Indians, and they never have a moment of regret." He lifted his eyes to Sean, "I don't know if you're a student of history, but whenever one race wants to subdue another, they first make their own people believe the others are less than human, then they make the subjugated people dependent on their handouts or control, and then they take everything from them, including their dignity. That is what the white man is doing now, both to the natives and with the war in the east, to the slaves."

Sean looked at the man, "The way you make it sound, it's hopeless! But I read about the Greeks, Romans, Mongols, Vikings, and others, and where are those mighty nations now? My worry is not history, but right now. And doing whatever I can to save some lives, red and white. Now, here's what I would like you to do. You say Standing Elk is your wife's father, then . . ." and Sean began to lay out a plan that had been working in his mind. Hopefully, it would be a plan that could prevent the theft of the supplies, or at least make sure they ended up in the hands of the right people.

CHAPTER TWENTY-FIVE
CONSPIRACY

"MEN, THERE'S SOMETHING YOU ALL NEED TA' KNOW 'bout." Bucky was speaking to the gathered men of the freight wagons. Twenty-six men sat before him, using every available object for seating. Two men were atop the near freighter, three lined out on the long tongue, a pair leaned on the front wheel, and others used boxes, logs, and rocks for their chair of choice. They were a haggard bunch, none concerned about his appearance with whiskers, dirt, and torn attire being the common look. Most tended towards a burly build, having developed the strength loading and unloading freighters, man-handling stubborn mules, and often tangling with one another. As he looked at the expectant group, he withdrew the folded telegram and began to read.

The men were attentive, but as soon as he finished, they began to ask questions. "So, who's goin' to Julesburg and who's goin' back to Independence?"

"You'll stay on the same wagons. If your wagon has been or will be unloaded and is not carryin' pelts and furs, you'll be goin' back to Missoura. If you're drivin' one o' the three pair that ain't yet unloaded, you'll be goin' south."

"What if we don't wanna go south?" asked another.

"If you can get someone to swap wit'cha, then do it."

Several of the men were talking among themselves, and Bucky overheard the word *gold* mentioned more than once. As he thought, there would be some that would get gold fever and want to stay in the gold fields and try their luck.

One of the teamsters spoke up, "Which way you goin', Bucky?"

He dropped his head, chuckled, "I've been south, all the way to Sante Fe, and I got fam'ly back in Missoura, so, I'm goin' east!"

"What about the war?" asked one of the men with the remuda.

"Well, Jonesy, ain't nobody knows what's goin' to happen wit' the war. Personal, I don't think it'll last much longer, no more'n a couple months anyway. But'chu cain't never tell about some folks. When you got a bunch o' folks shootin' at each other, one gets mad, th'other gets even, and it just keeps goin'. So, nobody knows."

"When we gonna leave out?" asked the one known as Slim, probably the biggest man in the crowd.

"Me'n Charlie's gonna talk 'bout that tonight. But we still got a couple wagons to get unloaded, so prob'ly soon."

The men began to drift off to their individual bedrolls, but most gathered in twos and threes to discuss what they wanted to do. Bucky knew the conniving and finagling that would take place as each man jockeyed for his choice of destination. The whisper of gold entered every conversation, for men that have never had wealth always long for it and the possibility of getting their own fortune was very appealing. Those that found themselves in the favored place of commanding the freighters that had not been unloaded and would be bound for Julesburg, realized they could barter for just about anything to surrender their place on their freighters. Promises and pleas were already being offered, and others had yet to decide what they had to offer and if they wanted to try their luck in the goldfields. At least with the freighters, they had a regular job and money coming in, and if they didn't know anything about mining for gold, they could be risking everything on the promise of nothing.

Charlie Canterbury leaned down to pour himself a cup of coffee, sat on an empty wooden crate, and looked to Bucky. "So, am I gonna be goin' with the wagons to Julesburg?"

"Maybe. But there's somethin' you need to know." He waved the telegram before him, "The Injuns know 'bout this!"

"They know?! How?!"

"Compliments of Captain Steele and the so'jers, I reckon. But they know, and they ain't none too happy 'bout it, neither!"

"Whooeee, that's worse'n spittin' in yer beer! What'chu reckon they'll do?"

"Hmmph, tryin' to figger what these Injuns'll do ain't no easier'n tryin' to figger what's gonna happen with the war! How'm I s'posed to know?!" declared Bucky. But after his talk with Sean, he had a pretty good idea that the Lakota would not allow the wagons to leave with any of the goods that were marked for the people. "What I do know is they got more'n five hundred warriors round'chere," nodding with his head toward the Indian encampments around the fort, "and there ain't even a hunnert so'jers in the fort. So, you figger it out!"

Bucky poured himself another cup of coffee, sat on the bench by the wagon wheel and leaned back against the spokes. He looked to Charlie, both men trying to think of a way to do what their employer, Harris and Lafferty, the Independence bankers, wanted and what the Indian Commissioner ordered, and not get their scalp lifted.

Charlie said, "Comin' out, we didn't have no trouble with any other tribe. I mean, we saw some Pawnee, maybe some Sioux, but none of 'em wanted to tangle with our bunch."

"No, because most huntin' parties only have at most a couple dozen warriors an' the numbers weren't in their favor. But," and he motioned around the camp, "The numbers here are shorely in their favor!"

Charlie shook his head, staring into the low flames of the fire, thinking. He looked up at the dark sky, black clouds obscuring the stars, and down to Bucky. "What if we were to leave at night?"

Bucky looked at him, thought about it, "You mean, try to sneak out without 'em knowin' 'bout it?"

"That's right. Sneak out!"

"Do you really think we can get twenty wagons, a hunnert mules, an' more to sneak out quietly? Them wagons and mules make more noise'n a brass band in the big city! We'd wake up ever' Injun, ever' so'jer, and ever'thing else if we tried that!" declared Bucky.

"But what if we just took the three sets of loaded wagons out. You know, we could even lead the teams an' keep 'em quiet. When we get away from the fort, we'd climb up and move out."

"If them Lakota found out, there'd only be what, six or eight of you against all them?"

Charlie leaned back, sipping his java, and thinking. "But if we made it away, and they didn't know it cuz the other wagons would still be here, maybe they'd just think we was in the fort unloadin'! Then we could wait for you down the trail an' we'd make it alright. Cuz, don't we hafta go back to the confluence of the North and South Platte to take the south route to Julesburg?"

"Yeah, course there ain't much at Julesburg, it's just a way station for the new stage line to the goldfields," answered Bucky. But he was also thinking about his conversation with Sean and what he was going to do about the missing wagons. Yet, Bucky had to be thinking about his commitment to his employer, Harris and Lafferty. He had contracted to deliver the goods to Fort Laramie and return with any traded pelts and hides from both Laramie and Bernard. He had the responsibility for the goods, the equipment, and the lives of the men. And the other side of the coin was Sean's commitment to do what was right, and that meant the Lakota were due the goods in all the wagons, even if the commissioner and his employers were determined to make an illegal profit at the expense of the Indians.

"I think we can do it!" declared Charlie, always the thoughtful one. "If I take the three pair out after midnight, and we push 'em through the next day, we can make it to the Narrows, where the North Platte makes that big bend back on itself by that long butte with all the alkali. You know the place, we camped there on the way out. We can wait for the rest of you there, and from then on there'd be 'nuff of us to fight off any war party they send! After all, we've all got Sharps an' there's 'nuff rifles in the wagons, we can be loaded fer bear!"

"Maybe. But let's think on it a spell." He looked to Charlie, thought a moment, "When would you wanna leave, tonight or tomorrow?"

"Could you have the rest of the wagons ready to leave sometime tomorrow? I don't wanna be out there too long 'fore you get there," observed Charlie.

"Maybe. If we get the rest of the men busy, we might get away 'bout noon. Don't know if we could catch up till the next day, but that'd be 'bout as soon as we could do it." He paused a moment, considering, "Well, let's find out who's gonna be goin'. I think there was some finagling goin' on," suggested Bucky as he rose from his seat, tossed aside the dregs of the coffee, and started for the group of bedrolls to talk to the men.

CHAPTER TWENTY-SIX
CLANDESTINE

THE NIGHT WAS CLEAR AND COOL. THE SENTINELS OF THE black sky flashed their beacons to one another in the mysterious messages of the heavens and the crescent moon held court over the western darkness. The nocturnal creatures fell silent, and the stillness awakened the black beast that lay beside Sean. He lifted his head, taking in the quiet and the smells; on padded feet, the shadowy figure peered over the crest of the riverbank to investigate the movement where there should be none. His orange eyes pierced the blanket of darkness, and a low growl parted his lips above the white fangs. He quickly went to the side of the sleeping figure and with a cold nose, nudged Sean awake.

Sean's eyes scanned the camp, looked to the horses and saw heads up, ears pricked, and eyes wide. He slowly turned his head to see Indy facing the edge of the river-bank that separated their camp from the fort. The wolf stood tense, watching, and quickly turned his head to see what was keeping Sean. Sean slipped from his blankets, rifle in hand and in a crouch followed Indy to the edge of the bank.

In the blackness, a long line of shadows moved away from the encampment and along the trail that paralleled the river. Sean bellied down and watched. He picked up on the distinct smell of mules, the leather of the harnesses, and as he listened, he heard the rustle of the many steps. A creak cried into the darkness and told of the turning of the big wheels of a loaded freighter. He puzzled about what he was seeing, thinking he should hear the rattle of trace chains, but realized the muleskinners must have wrapped the chains in rags or something to quiet the give-away rattle. Suddenly, the tall freighters moved under the crescent of the moon, as the dim moonlight outlined the silhouettes of two coupled wagons. Those were followed closely by another long line of mule teams, led by two men walking at their heads.

When the last of the three doubled freighters passed, Sean slipped back to his camp and started saddling the horses. A whisper came from his shoulder, "I put the coffee pot on the coals; it will be warm soon."

Fox rolled up their blankets and started gathering the other camp gear. As she packed the panniers, Sean poured himself some coffee, took a deep sip, and poured another cup for Fox. He smiled as he thought of how quickly she had taken to the coffee and shared his desire for a cup of the hot brew to start the day. They stashed their cups in a pannier, mounted up, and took to the trail following the escaping freighters.

Indy stretched out as he loped beside the trail. He scanned all around, his practiced eyes missing nothing. He ignored the big-footed jackrabbit that ducked behind a clump of greasewood, watched a skinny coyote scamper toward a lonely cedar, and glanced at the feathered vanguard that sent his question bouncing across the plains. He was in his element and enjoying every moment, and a quick glance over his shoulder told of the nearness of his people. When a lonesome wail from a distant butte told of a she-wolf looking for company, Indy stopped, looked in the direction of the howl, lifted his voice to answer.

Fox looked to Sean, "That sent chills down my back! Will he stay with us?"

"That's his choice. He's left before, like when he went after the pack that attacked you, but he has always come back. I hope he stays, but . . ." and Sean shrugged his shoulders as the pair looked at the dark shadow they knew was their friend. Orange eyes that seemed to glow in the dark turned their way, then Indy's head dropped as he took to the trail again.

The North Platte carved its way through the empty prairie, always moving to the east south-east, as if it was bound to the rising sun. When old Sol finally showed his face, the bright gold of morning bounced its rays off the rippling water, and the light was almost blinding as Sean and Fox followed the dusty trail of the disappearing wagons. Daylight revealed several low-rising, flat-top mesas off to their right, and the meandering North Platte farther away from the trail off their left shoulder. The wagon road had taken a more direct route across the wide flats and would soon join the greener slopes that dropped into the river.

Sean nodded toward a herd of antelope that watched the passing duo with their horses and the big black wolf.

Suddenly, the herd buck turned away, goading his follow-ers, and the entire bunch took off at a run toward the distant buttes. Sean asked, "You like Antelope meat?"

Fox cocked her head to the side, "It makes good pemmican, but I like deer meat better, especially those that feed by the river."

Sean chuckled, "Yeah, when they don't eat anything but what's out here on the prairie, buffalo grass, grama, sage, and more, they don't taste as good. I guess that green stuff by the water is better." He thought for a moment, "Maybe I'll try to get us a nice tender doe this evenin', what say?"

"Ummm, and maybe I'll find some more Camas or turnips to go with it!" She smiled, knowing Sean had enjoyed her Camas bulbs before.

"Alright now, you're making me hungry already. How 'bout we stop for some coffee and give the horses a little graze?"

The trail had dropped below a slight bluff and came near a bend in the river. With cottonwoods, alder, willows, and more, they easily found shade from the morning sun and grass for the horses. As Fox gathered some dry sticks for a small fire, Sean took the telescope from his saddlebags and started for the bluff. He motioned to Fox where he was going, and with a nod, she turned back to her preparations.

Indy and Sean sat down atop the bluff, searching the distance all around for any sign of life or danger. Their promontory was about a hundred feet above the valley floor and the river, and only slightly above the level of the plains, but it offered a view of the trail and river as it pointed to the southeast. He brought his knees up, rested his elbows to support the scope, and scanned the distant trail. They had purposely taken their time, not wanting to be too close behind the wagons to be seen, but near enough to keep them within reach. Since they took to the trail in the night, Sean had been thinking about how he might turn them back and had dismissed most ideas. He now pondered about the possibilities, knowing there would be eight or ten men with the wagons, two for each double hook-up, a couple of outriders, and maybe one or two to help or take care of the mules. And there was just him and Fox.

He couldn't see the wagons, but as he searched, he spotted a wispy dust cloud above the trail. He estimated they were no more than five miles, perhaps less, away. They could overtake them easily, but a direct confrontation could be deadly, and his goal was for no bloodshed. He looked again, scanned the terrain, and after rubbing Indy behind his ears, the two friends started down the slope, Sean digging his heels into the loose soil as he tried to keep up with Indy.

"Did you see them?" asked Fox as she poured Sean a cup of coffee. She handed him a left-over Johnny Cake, heated on the stone beside the fire, and a handful of pemmican, seating herself next to him and waiting for an answer.

"Yeah, not more'n five miles, maybe less. They've been pushin' purty hard, and I think we'll wait till first thing in the mornin' 'fore we do anything."

"And what will we do?"

"Not sure yet. Just have to take our time, see how they camp, think on it a spell, and try to figger out sumpin' that won't get us killed."

"I would not like that," declared Fox, stoically.

"Me neither," answered Sean, grinning. "So, I guess we'll just have to be mighty careful 'bout things. There's prob'ly eight to ten of 'em, but I don't think they'll be expectin' anything. So . . ." drawled Sean, shrugging his shoulders and taking another drink of coffee.

The horses had been watered and were now enjoying the lush green grass on the riverbank as Sean reclined back to rest on his elbows and looked to Fox. "What'd your ma have to say about you an' me, you know, getting hitched?

"Hitched?" asked Fox, wondering at this man's strange words.

"Uh, I guess your people call it 'Joined.'"

Fox laughed, "She is happy. She said she knew that would happen, even before I left to follow you."

"Yeah, that's a mother for you. They always seem to know what's gonna happen." He tossed the dregs aside, stood up and started for the horses. He looked over his shoulder to Fox, "I'd like to catch up with the wagons, maybe get ahead of 'em, 'fore we camp tonight."

CHAPTER TWENTY-SEVEN
CONFRONTATION

THE LONG ROW OF GULLEY CUT BUTTES MARCHED IN formation toward the meeting with the sharp bend of the North Platte. With their uniformed shoulders marked with strips of green interspersed with the pale colors of white feldspar, the buttes appeared to be equal in size and distance with each other as they covered the parade ground of the prairie. Yet, at the end of the formation, a wide draw filled with alder and willows, masked the camp of Sean and Fox. Dusk had almost set when Sean came back into camp, the carcass of a young doe over his shoulders. Fox smiled as Sean dropped his burden and went to the stack of gear to put his longbow back in the sheath and set his quiver beside it.

They were downwind and downstream from the camp of the freighters and had no concern about their camp being discovered. Fox prepared a fine meal and afterwards when they sat on a log, side by side, Sean said, "I think I'm gonna go into their camp tonight, after they're asleep, and see if I can't get most of their rifles and such, before we confront them."

Fox looked at Sean, dropped her eyes, and thought about what he planned. She remembered how easily he snuck into camp of the Crow and she thought it would be easier to do the same with these men, but it was still very risky. She breathed deeply, looked at him, and asked, "What if we both did it, together?"

He looked at her, thought of her sneaking in among some sleeping white men, and quickly dismissed the idea. "No, I think I would rather have you up on a bluff with that Sharps in case I get caught. That way, maybe you can rescue me, if I need it!" he chuckled at the thought and smiled at Fox.

———

PODUNK WAS the hostler who doubled as cook and the men had come to appreciate his ability over the cookfire. He wasn't a big man by any measure, but he was known as a scrapper and when one of the muleskinners hollered, "Hey, Podunk! Bring me some more vittles!"

The cook answered, "Get it yourself! I just cook it, I ain't gonna serve it!"

The skinner was the one known as Slim and was the biggest of the crew and was used to intimidating others into acceding to his demands, and when this little man sassed him back, he roared and came to his feet and stomped toward Podunk. He was within a couple of steps of the cook when the flash of a Bowie knife passed in front of his face and the big blade stuck in the side of the freighter at the man's side. The blade had come close enough to give him a shave if he had breathed at the wrong time and Slim jerked his head to the side to see Charlie Canterbury staring at him. The teamster boss glared and growled, "Don't you even think about touching Podunk! Every man here will have your hide! If we lose him, then we go hungry, and hunger is somethin' that don't agree with me!"

Slim looked at Charlie, back at the knife that still trembled in the wood of the freighter, and mumbled, "Uh, sure Charlie. I was just gonna get me some more vittles!"

"You forgot your plate!" growled Charlie, nodding towards Slim's plate, still sitting by his perch.

"Uh, yeah," replied Slim and went back for the tin.

Charlie walked to the freighter, pulled his knife out and replaced it in its sheath at his belt. The other skinners were lounging around the fire, listless and tired from the long day's drive. Charlie asked the one known as Skunk because of the streak of white through his black hair, "Say Skunk, how 'bout gettin' us a couple jugs of that 'medicine' in that crate at the front of your wagon." Charlie knew taking alcohol of any kind into Indian territory was strictly against army regulations and the law of the territory, but the presence of several cases of the 'medicine' was proof to Charlie that Harris and Lafferty never had any intention of the contents of these wagons ever making it into the hands of the Lakota. But whiskey in the goldfields would be worth its weight in gold. In the meantime, they could use a little themselves.

When Skunk returned, he had a broad smile and a bottle in each hand and one under each arm. "Now this is what I call medicine! How'dju know that's what it was?" he asked Charlie.

"I looked!"

"But Bucky said we couldn't do any drinkin' or take any liquor with us!"

"Yeah, well, Bucky's a teetotaler, I ain't. After the long day we just spent, I think we could all use a drink."

"Hear, hear!" came the cry of all the men around the fire, each reaching out their coffee cups to be filled. One man asked, "What about when Bucky catches up with us?"

Charlie laughed, "We're drinkin' the evidence! How's he gonna know!"

The remark was greeted by laughter and the tired men were re-energized with the whiskey. Four bottles among ten thirsty men did not last long and when they wanted more, Charlie insisted they all turn in because the others would join them tomorrow and they needed clear heads for the coming journey. The orders were met with considerable grumbling, but all the men were tired and anxious for their bedrolls.

———

WHEN SEAN SCOUTED the freighters from the bluff on their way to their camp, he mentally marked the different wagons; one held the cook gear, one held the bedrolls of the men, and the others were loaded to the brim with boxes and crates. Now, in the black of night, he slowly made his approach. He had watched the camp for any indication of guards or lookouts, but none were seen, and he shook his head at the carelessness of men camping in Indian territory and presuming they were safe with their numbers and posted no one on lookout. How easy it would be for a war party to steal all the mules and horses and most of their scalps without anyone knowing it until daylight. With the wagons parked away from any trees or other cover, Sean had to belly down and crawl through the bunch-grass.

When he was near the closest wagon, he slowly rose to his feet and, in a crouch, drew nearer. He stood next to a wagon, listening. In the distance, the murmuring of the slow flowing river provided the accompaniment of the occasional harping cry of a nighthawk. He heard the croak of frogs as they nestled into the mud at the edge of the water. But the prominent sound was the out of tune chorus of snoring freighters. With an occasional snort as someone rolled over, the rattle and cluck and grumble of the unkempt men continued uninterrupted. He slowly moved around the end of the wagon, bent low to see one man on his side, arms at his chest and back to Sean, mumbling in his sleep, something about Mary. Sean shook his head and slowly reached for the man's rifle lying near his head. He lifted the heavy Sharps and stepped back beside the wagon. He realized he had been holding his breath and slowly exhaled. Sean had noted when he watched the group earlier, they had used the coupled wagon behind where he stood for the bedrolls. He stepped up to look in, but the darkness yielded nothing. He reached down into the bed, felt around for a blanket and placed the rifle down quietly. His long leg reached down to touch the ground, and he looked for his next target.

The smell of whiskey was strong, and Sean wondered if it had been medicinally applied to a wound or if the men had been on a binge. As he moved among them, every man had the smell of liquor and Sean smiled at the thought, wondering if God was watching out for him by using the devil's brew. Not everyone had a rifle nearby, but Sean relieved most of the men of their weapons, whether rifles or pistols, and hid them in the wagon, covering them with a blanket, knowing they would not expect to find them there. It was more than likely that he missed some weapons, but most were now hidden in the wagon. It had taken him most of an hour, but with one last look around, he was satisfied with his night's work.

———

SEAN HAD EXPLAINED his plan to Fox, emphasizing where she was to be and the signals he would give and asked if she understood or had any questions. She looked up at her man, smiled and shook her head. Sean looked to her, seeing her as a tiny frail figure of a woman that he was sending on a mission most men would not undertake. "You sure you wanna do this?"

"Yes. I am ready," she declared as she mounted her paint pony. Her Sharps was in the scabbard and the possibles bag hung over one shoulder. Her bow was in a sheath beneath her left saddle fender and the quiver of arrows hung behind her leg. She bent down and kissed her man, reined around to leave, when Sean said, "I'll give you plenty of time. And don't forget to move around!"

She waved at him and started back up the line of buttes, keeping the knobs between her and the river bottom. When he had allowed what he deemed would be sufficient time, he swung aboard Dusty and started back toward the wagons. They had passed the train after dusk last night, and Sean took the time to scout their location and positioning before he formulated the plan. He whispered a prayer, "Lord, you know what needs to be done. We just wanna do what's right and try to keep the Lakota from makin' war on these folks. So, I'm askin' for you to take charge of this and use me as You see fit! Thanks Lord. Amen." He looked down at Indy, reined up and with a wide sweeping gesture, sent the wolf to circle the wagons by coming from the river's edge. Once the wolf disappeared into the brush, Sean gigged Dusty forward.

The sun was yet to make its full debut, but the early morning light tinted the trees and slopes with shades of pink and orange. Sean neared the wagons and when about fifty yards out, he paused and called out, "Hello the camp!" He waited for an answer or some sign of life. Nothing happened. He called out again, "Hello the camp! I'm comin' in and I'm friendly!" It was one of the many unwritten laws of the frontier, a man should never approach a camp without announcing himself and waiting for an invitation. Anything less would usually get a man shot. He gigged Dusty forward slowly, stopped again about thirty yards out, held up both hands as he called again, "Hello the camp!"

Finally, a whiskered face peered around the corner of a wagon, hair tousled and rubbing his eyes as he pulled galluses over his shoulders. He looked at Sean, one man alone, and Sean hollered again, "Hello. I'm friendly and looking for coffee. Got'ny?"

Whisker face grunted and waved Sean forward. He turned his back on the visitor and stumbled toward the coals of the night before. Sean stepped down, tethered

Dusty to a big wheel of the nearest freighter, careful to make certain the horse was well to the side away from the bluff. He watched as Whiskers grabbed up a big blue enamel coffee pot, shook it, and turned toward one of the freighters to go to the water barrel to refill the pot. Sean walked to the coals, picked up a couple of sticks from a small stack and stirred the embers before dropping the smaller sticks to get the fire rekindled.

Whiskers returned and sat the full pot at the edge of the coals, dropped down on a long shipping container and looked to Sean. "Travelin' alone are ya'?"

"I don't think a man is ever really alone out here," said Sean, motioning to the wilderness, "Do you?"

Whiskers scowled at Sean, mumbled, "I don't reckon. Where ya' bound?"

"Fort Laramie, you?"

The scruffy man seemed to relax a little, chuckled, "Goin' to the goldfields down south. Gonna make muh fortune!"

Sean looked at the man, cocked his head to the side and asked, "All y'all?"

"Nah, some'r just drivin' the wagons and they'll take 'em back to Independence. Not me! I'm tryin' for some o' that gold folks're talkin' 'bout!"

As the two men talked, waiting for the coffee, others began to roll out and make their way to the bushes before returning to the fire, to also wait for coffee. One by one they looked at Sean, but no one spoke as each man groaned and mumbled as he found a seat near the fire. Each man stared at the coffee pot, trying to will it to be done, as they fingered their empty cups, some cradling their heads in their hands. Sean had fully expected some of the men to come from their blankets shouting about their rifles missing, but no one thought about their rifles, they were too intent on getting some coffee.

When the pot started to rattle its lid, Whiskers snatched up a bag of ground coffee and flipped the lid back on the pot, pouring in three handfuls of coffee. He grabbed a stick to flip the lid back over and sat back to stare at the pot with the others. Sean looked around the group, said, "You fellas look like somethin' the cat drug in, what happened?"

The big man, Slim, looked up at Sean, "Who're you?"

Sean chuckled, "Just a passerby, beggin' a cup o' coffee."

Whiskers explained, "We had a touch o' whiskey last night. Been too long between drinks and it kinda done us in."

Sean looked around, "Maybe you need some hair of the dog that bit'chu?"

Grumbles went around the group and one man staggered up and pushed away from the group heading for the bushes, but didn't quite make it, leaving his stomach's contents by the big rear wheel of a freighter. His action met with a few moans and complaints, but when Whiskers poured a bit of cold water into the coffee pot to settle the grounds, they all reached for their cups. Sean waited his turn, watching each of the men, judging who might be the one who would resist the most. In any group, there was always a leader, whether assigned or assumed, and if the leader could be quelled, the others would follow.

When he was finally given access to the pot, he poured himself a cup and stood to one side, watching each of the men. They were a scruffy lot, but Sean knew muleskinners and roustabouts were also a tough bunch of men. They would not easily be cowed, but he had to try.

CHAPTER TWENTY-EIGHT
CONSTERNATION

THE GRUMBLING CONTINUED BUT PODUNK STARTED FIXING some breakfast, and the smell of sizzling pork belly sent a few more to the bushes. The evening before, Podunk had gathered a hatful of duck eggs and he was whipping them together in a large tin bowl. Sean stood to the side, sipping his coffee and listening to the snippets of conversation that passed around the circle.

"How long ya' reckon it'll take us to get to the gold-fields?" asked a man with a laurel of hair just above his ears that accented his bald pate.

"Charlie said it was four days or so to the meetin' of the waters for th' North an' South Platte, an' 'nother week after we leave Julesburg. That'll leave us plenty time to find a claim an' work it 'fore the snow falls," declared his friend, tugging at his galluses.

"You know anythin' 'bout minin' gold?"

"Nah, but they's sayin' it's just layin' aroun' and all we gotta do is find it! Cain't be too hard, can it?"

Sean shook his head at the gullibility of the average

man, knowing the nature of men was to find something for nothing. Yet Sean had learned at an early age that nothing worth having is easy on the come. His pa taught him that hard work was its own reward and a lazy man's doin' usually brought him to poor ends. He sucked in a deep breath and shrugged his shoulders and walked away from the group near the wagon. He crossed to the other side of the fire and sat on the corner of a crate held down by Charlie Canterbury. Sean asked, "I take it you're the leader of this bunch?" nodding his head toward the gathering of teamsters.

"That's right, well mostly. Charlie's muh name, yours?'

Sean chuckled, "Well, 'round here'bouts, I'm known as Bear Chaser, but muh given name is Sean. But you said 'mostly'?"

"Yeah, we're waitin' fer the rest of our outfit comin' from Laramie. The ramrod o' the bunch is with them. Then we'll be movin' on."

"Some o' the fellas were talkin' 'bout the goldfields, is ever'body goin'?" inquired Sean.

"Nah, just this bunch, but we figgered it'd be safer travelin' together till we get outta Sioux country."

"Got a point there, but it'd prob'ly be safer for y'all to just hook up and head back to the Fort."

Charlie scowled at Sean, "What'chu mean?"

Sean stood and casually moved away from the fire and turned to look back at a frowning Charlie, "Well, since your cargo belongs to the Lakota and they're comin' after it, if they thought you were takin' it back to 'em instead o' stealin' it, they might decide not to stretch you out on them wheels there and skin you alive, like they been known to do when they're a mite upset."

Charlie jumped to his feet, looking around at the bluffs and the trees by the river, "What'chu mean, I don't see no Injuns! Wh . . .who are you anyhow?" He had stepped closer to Sean and puffed out his chest as he snarled the words. "How d'you know 'bout our cargo and the Injuns?" he shouted, still looking around for any attackers.

Sean held up an open palm before the man, motioning him to back off, "I'm the scout from Laramie, and all the chiefs know about the telegram from the commissioner. They gave me time to convince you to turn around before they come after you, but to be honest, they didn't think I could do it!"

"You're the scout? Why would you take sides wit' them savages?" he fumed, shifting his weight from one foot to the other, balled fists at his sides. Several of the other men were now standing behind Charlie, angry stares focused on Sean.

Sean knew the crowd would explode at the slightest provocation, and he hoped a warning would get their attention. He casually reached up to remove his hat as if to wipe the sweat from his brow. Almost simultaneously, the coals of the fire exploded, and an echoing boom came from the bluff. All the men jumped, but Podunk jumped higher and screamed louder than all the rest. He kept screaming as he dived under the nearest wagon, only to be pushed aside by two others. Some dropped into a crouch, others dove for cover beneath or behind the wagons. One man shouted, "Hey! Where's muh rifle?" His cry was mimicked by others as they searched their bedrolls for their weapons.

"Who took it!" shouted one.

"Alright, where is it? I know it was here when I turned in!"

Other cries of alarm were sounded as the men searched for their weapons yet trying to keep under cover and behind the wagons.

Sean stood, unalarmed, sipping his coffee as the others scampered about. Charlie shouted at him from beside a wagon, "Ain't'chu gonna take cover?"

"Why? They're not shootin' at me. I didn't take their supplies!"

"This is your doin', ain't it?" demanded Charlie. "Where'd you put our rifles? An' when did you take 'em?" pleaded the exasperated teamster.

"Yup. I took 'em. It was purty easy with all you drunks snoring last night."

"I oughta tear you apart with my bare hands!" growled Charlie. Some of the other men shouted, "Do it! Kill him, Charlie!"

Others hollered, "Wait'll we get our rifles back!"

Charlie started for Sean, fists clenching and unclenching, snarling like a mad dog. He had always had his way by threatening or bullying, seldom did it result in an actual fight. But the times he had fought were rough and tumble on the docks at the warehouse. With his head slightly tilted, he stomped forward, "Get those rifles, NOW!" he demanded.

Sean grinned, and looked at the man like he was an oddity, then answered, "Nope. But if you get the teams hooked up and get these wagons turned around, I might be able to call them," nodding his head toward the bluffs, "off."

"Then I'll beat it outta yuh!" roared Charlie as he dropped into a crouch, arms wide, and stomped closer.

Sean reached for his hat, doffed it to toss it aside, when the big Sharps boomed again, and the bullet plowed dirt just in front of Charlie. The big man jumped back, looked with wide eyes to the bluff. "I still don't see any Injuns! I think it's a bluff!"

Sean casually stripped off his belt with the holstered Colt and Tomahawk, laid them aside and stepped back, and with his open hands wide at his side, he invited Charlie, "C'mon then."

Charlie took one careful step, looked back to the bluff, then to his men. The teamsters shouted, "Take him Charlie!" and the man charged, roaring like a mad bull. He swung a roundhouse, expecting to take Sean's head off, but Sean ducked under, and brought up a hard fist from the ground as he pivoted, bringing all his weight behind it. He buried his fist in the angry man's belly and as he slumped forward, Sean brought a hatchet chop fist to the right side of the man's head, bringing blood from his ear.

Charlie stumbled forward, catching his balance as he turned, surprised at the younger man that introduced himself with such a blow. The teamster bent his knees and brought his fists up before his face, looking between them at Sean and began to circle to his left. Sean went to the balls of his feet, held his hands loosely before his chest, watching the man's eyes. Charlie bobbed his head to one side, feinted with his left and started a punch with his right. Sean ducked under the right, but the glancing blow caught him high on the cheek, splitting skin and bringing blood. Sean wiped his face, staggered as step and feinted with his left. When the teamster ducked away, Sean brought his right to the man's wind, followed by his left as he repeatedly pounded the man's middle. Charlie staggered back, wind-milling his arms to catch himself. Sean stepped in with a straight left to the teamster's face and felt his nose crunch and his teeth give way. Sean stepped back, watched Charlie drop his head and spit blood and a tooth. When he stood back up, his face was covered with blood, but anger flared from his eyes.

The muleskinner roared again and charged, arms wide, wanting to get Sean in a bear-hug, but Sean went to the ground, throwing all his weight at the man's feet and the burly figure fell face forward. Sean rolled out from under the thrashing legs and came quickly to his feet. Charlie came to all fours and stood to turn and face Sean, just as Sean waded into him, head down, and pummeling the man in the wind repeatedly. Charlie took the beating, then wrapped his arms around Sean's arms and chest, leaned back to lift him off the ground, but the younger man arched his back, then brought his forehead smashing into the bloody pulp of the teamster's nose. Charlie dropped his arms and put his hand to his face as he bent over to let the blood drip to the ground. But Sean waded in again, bringing an uppercut from the ground and pivoted to put all his force and weight behind it. When he connected with his chin, the big man staggered back, tripping over his own feet, and floundered as he hit the ground, to roll to his stomach, moaning.

No one moved as Sean went to the water barrel at the side of the wagon and with the dipper, poured water over his head. He wiped his face and flipped back his hair as he walked to the box where his belt lay. Most of the men just watched, but Whiskers had slipped from under his wagon and picked up his muleskinner bullwhip. He uncoiled the long whip, and called out to Sean, "You! Scout!"

Sean turned back toward the man, his belt and holster hanging from his hand, and the whip lashed out and cracked at Sean's shoulder, cutting through the buckskin, bringing blood and making Sean wince as he dropped his belt and pistol. He grabbed at his shoulder and saw Whiskers bringing the long whip back and forward for another strike. Sean lifted his arm over his head and dropped to his knees. The popper cracked across his back, again cutting the buckskin and bringing blood as Sean arched his back in pain.

The men shouted, "Yeah! Cut him up!" and more. Sean turned quickly, searching for his belt and pistol and tomahawk, but they were out of reach. He came to his feet and his hand went over his shoulder to reach for the Bowie at his back, but suddenly a black shadow came from between the wagons. Indy launched himself at the man with the whip, catching his forearm just as Whiskers started to bring it forward to strike again. But the long fangs were buried deep in his flesh as the big wolf bore his prey to the ground. He ripped at the screaming man's forearm, tore his fangs free, and with both front paws on the man's chest, blood dripping from his teeth, the wolf growled and snapped his jaws. The man brought his uninjured arm across his face, still screaming and Indy grabbed that arm in a vice-like grip, sinking his teeth to the bone.

Sean hollered at the black wolf and Indy froze, but did not free the man's arm. A deep growl came from deep in his chest and his orange eyes flamed. Another shout from Sean, and Indy tore his fangs from the man's arm, ripping flesh, and in an instant, he was off the man and trotted easily to Sean's side. He stood close, but at an attack stance, head lowered, eyes flaring, teeth showing under snarling lips. Sean dropped his arm to the scruff of the wolf's neck, spoke softly to him, and replaced his belt with the holstered Colt and Hawk.

He raised his voice, "Men, if you harness your mules and hook-up, we'll get started back to the fort. I advise you not to try anything because I'm purty sure you don't wanna know what it would be like to try to stop a .54 caliber slug from a Sharps rifle."

Slowly, the men crawled from their cover, started gathering up their bedrolls and began harnessing the mules. The teams were soon harnessed, hooked up, and ready. While they were busy at their task, Sean had Podunk bandaging the two injured men, placing them atop the packed crates on the first wagon. At Sean's signal, the lead wagon swung wide and started back leading the others towards Fort Laramie.

CHAPTER TWENTY-NINE
DESERTERS

"IT REALLY DOESN'T MAKE ANY DIFFERENCE WHAT YOU think, Lieutenant. Call it desertion if you like, but after what we've heard about this war, we are going to join the South!" He waved a telegram over his desk at the junior grade officer, "And by what my friend has said, I could get a commission with a rank as a colonel if I join the Confederates! We need officers and we need to train the thousands of men that are begging to get in the fight. I have always believed in the cause of the south, we don't need a bunch of big city northerners telling us what we can and can't do!"

Lieutenant Hood sat quietly, shaking his head. He looked up to Captain Steele, always had, since he had been assigned to the regiment at Fort Laramie, but he also believed in the discipline of the Army and honoring one's commitment. He lifted his eyes to Steele, "How many?"

"How many, what?"

"How many men are you taking with you?"

"Only 'bout a dozen. Sergeant O'Reilly, Sergeant

Watkins, and ten enlisted men. There are several others that are fence straddlers, but these are determined and would leave whether or not any others joined. But my classmate from West Point, Captain Smithfield, already committed to the South and has been given the rank of lieutenant colonel, with a promise of colonel when the regiment is trained."

"Well, that sounds good, but that means the two of us could face each other across the battlefield." He shook his head at the thought, "You've been too good a friend. I don't think I could shoot you. You know you'll be leavin' the rest of us at the mercy of the Lakota, don'tchu?"

"I don't think anything's gonna happen. The Scout, Sean, said he thought the Lakota will solve the problem themselves and not attack the fort. But even if we stayed, our handful wouldn't make a difference against five hundred or more warriors."

"No, prob'ly not. When you leavin'?" asked the Lieutenant.

"We'll leave 'bout mid-day. In full uniform so the Sioux will think we're goin' after the other wagons. Maybe that'll keep 'em off your back."

"Maybe." The junior officer stood and extended his hand. The two men shook hands, and Lieutenant Hood turned and left the office. The Captain watched his friend leave, his shoulders sagged as he realized the gravity of his decision, but he was resolved to follow his conscience and join the south. He left all the papers in the office, taking only his personal belongings, a tintype of his wife, two personal letters, the telegram, and his battle sword. With a last look around, he walked from the office, turned toward the livery, and prepared to pack his gear for the trip.

———

It wasn't a meeting of the council, but these men were all war leaders of their bands. Standing Elk and Red Cloud of the Oglala, Little Thunder of the Brulé, Touch the Clouds of the Miniconjou, and Thomas Twiss, the agent turned Oglala.

"The wagons with the rifles and powder are gone!" declared Little Thunder, looking around the circle.

Red Cloud added, "You," pointing to Twiss, "said we were to give the scout time. It has been three suns and they have not returned."

Standing Elk added, "The sister of my woman heard the soldiers talk in the trader's that many will be leaving to join the white man war in the east. She could not say for sure, but she thought they were going to take the wagons that left and the rifles they carried to the white man's war."

Twiss asked, "Have any soldiers left the fort?"

As each man looked to one another, none were able to answer the question.

"Then let me tell you what the scout had planned," he began. As he spoke, each of the war leaders listened, sometimes nodding understanding and agreement. When he was finished, he looked to his wife's father, Standing Elk and asked, "Would you lead the others in this?"

Standing Elk looked from one to the other and said, "Red Cloud, we," motioning to himself and the other war leader, "will do this."

———

THE REST of the wagons had left the fort at first light. It was late morning when the deserters began to assemble by the livery. Captain Steele drew them together and explained, "We'll leave as if we are a regular detail on a mission. Full uniform, and in formation. One man will follow with the wagon, so be sure to put your bedrolls and personal gear in before we load the supplies."

"If we take a wagon and supplies, won't that be stealin'?" asked a greenhorn recruit.

"I have signed us out on a scouting detail and the needed supplies are accounted for, but of course we won't be coming back, so, it won't be any different than if we were attacked by Indians or something like that," explained the Captain, feeling a little guilty at trying to explain away what was, in fact, thievery. He had always been an honest and moral man, but he justified his actions with the thought that war was neither honest nor moral; it was war.

MANY FROM THE encampments around the fort watched as the squad of soldiers rode through the massive gates. Most paid little attention as they busied themselves packing their newly received supplies in anticipation of their return to their summer camp far from the fort. One vigilant warrior trotted away toward one of the central lodges to give the report of the soldiers leaving.

———

SEAN RODE WELL AHEAD of the lead wagon and was deep in thought when he looked up to see Fox rise up from a low swale, leading the pack horse and coming toward him. Her broad smile brought one of his own as she swung her mount beside his, neither slowing. She grinned at him and asked, "Well?" waiting for some acknowledgement of her shooting at the wagons.

"You did fine."

She looked at the split on his cheek, scowled, "I will fix that when we stop."

"That's just it, I don't wanna stop, but I know we'll have to soon enough. None of these fellas are too happy about goin' back to the fort. I think some of 'em had plans for these supplies, like sellin' 'em to the miners or somethin'. So, when we stop, be careful and stay out of reach of any of those men."

WITH THE LATE START, Sean thought they would make it to the same location where he and Fox had stopped when they followed the wagons. The tall cluster of cottonwoods at the edge of the river marked the spot where there would be ample graze for the thirty and more mules. Sean and Fox made their camp apart from the freighters but when Podunk invited them to join the group for the meal, they accepted.

The setting sun had lengthened the shadows as the last of the day's light dimmed, when Sean and Fox approached the group seated near the fire. Sean had been suspicious of the invitation and had sent Indy through the trees to approach the camp from the riverbank. Podunk greeted them as they arrived, and several of the men nodded as they neared. While Fox walked toward the cook's table, two men that had been leaning against the front wheel of the freighter nearest the fire, suddenly grabbed at Sean thinking to overpower him. But Sean was quicker than they expected and used the weight of the man at his right against him, throwing him into the other attacker. But they quickly recovered and came at him again.

When the attack happened, Fox quickly kicked at the side of the cook's knee, dropping him instantly. She stepped away from the man, although he reached out for her. In one fluid move, she drew the Bowie from the scabbard at her back and threw it at Sean's bigger attacker. The big knife flashed in the light of the fire and surprised the bigger man as he reached for Sean. The knife was impaled in the side of the wagon, between his legs, it's razor sharp blade cutting the canvas britches at the crotch, making him stretch to his tiptoes. He sucked in his breath, afraid to move. He held his hand out toward the other attacker, pointed down to the knife, and stuttered, "Uh, uh, uh, . . ."

The instant of distraction allowed Sean to draw his Colt and he stuck the barrel under the chin of the second attacker, cocking the hammer with a click that captured the attention of every man at the fire. Fox held her new pocket Dragoon that Sean had just purchased at the fort Sutler, but she proudly displayed her dexterity with it as she pointed it at the circle of men and grinned. None of the men dared move, each one sitting back and holding their hands out as if they weren't a part of the attack.

Sean looked from one to the other, lifted his voice, "Indy!" The big wolf trotted from the shadows of the freighters to stand between Sean and Fox. He faced the men, mouth open and fangs showing, head lowered, ready to attack. All of the men involuntarily drew back as they looked at the wolf, knowing what he had done to Whiskers. Sean stepped back from his attacker, snatched the Bowie from the wagon board, and walked to Fox. He smiled at her as he handed her the knife and watched as she slipped it back into the scabbard hanging at her back. He looked to the men, "Sorry we won't be able to stay for the meal, but we'll be nearby if we're needed."

CHAPTER THIRTY
CONVERGENCE

"Cap'n, looks like we can go 'round them wagons. They're circlin' up to make camp, an' there's a long dry wash that'll keep us outta sight till we're past 'em."

"Sounds good, Sergeant. I want to reach the other freighters before the rest of these wagons catch up. If we're gonna take them for the south, we might have to do it after dark." The deserters had not planned to take the wagons, as all were anxious to clear out of the country and make it to the sympathetic southern states as soon as possible. But as the Captain considered the cargo of rifles, powder, lead, and other goods that could equip and feed a lot of soldiers, he believed the risk would be worth it. When they arrived with that bounty, it would go a long way towards gaining favor with those in command.

The sergeant rode back along the column of men instructing them, "Men, we've got to get around those wagons while it's still light. We're gonna be movin' through a dry wash and we can't be makin' any noise.

Make sure your canteens and anything else that makes noise is secured and no talking as we move, unnerstand?" He nodded to all the 'yes sergeant' responses and reined around to rejoin the captain. With a wave of his hand, the captain sent the sergeant into the lead to guide the column into the wash.

SEAN AND FOX made their camp about forty yards from the nearest wagon, enough distance to keep an eye on the men, but far enough to make it difficult for them to come into his camp unexpected. It was against a shear rock bluff at the edge of the buttes and surrounded by cottonwoods and alders. But the space for their bedrolls and cookfire also gave room for the tethered horses. Before their last confrontation with the teamsters, they had given their horses water and graze then picketed them near the camp.

As they turned into their blankets, one on each side of the fire, Fox leaned on her elbow looking to Sean, "Do you think they will try to come into our camp?"

"I doubt it, not with Indy on guard. I think he purty well struck the fear of God in their souls. I don't plan to do too much sleepin' nohow, so, it'll be alright. You get some rest, it's gonna be a long day tomorrow."

She smiled, lay back on her blanket, and answered, "Alright boyfriend," and giggled in the darkness.

Sean lay looking at the stars, remembering. There had been many times he and his father had sat on the top rail of the fence, looking at and learning about the stars. It seemed to be a family thing as his father and grandfather did the same. He marveled at the clear night and the crescent of the moon hanging high in the heavens. By early morning it would be nearing the western horizon, but now it appeared as the band leader and his orchestra. As he lay in the quiet, the frogs, cicadas, and coyotes sang their choruses while he talked to his Lord. But before he said 'Amen', the sounds of the night grew silent. He paused in his breathing, looked to the horses that stood facing toward the wagons, ears pricked and eyes wide. A quick glance saw Indy up and watching, tense, and alert. He slowly rolled out of his blankets, rifle in hand as he stealthily walked toward the trees at the edge of his camp.

He expected to see some of the teamsters trying to sneak up on his camp, but he saw no movement. His silhouette melded with the cottonwood as he watched, searching the dim light and the dark shadows for any movement. Moments later, from the edge of the bluff, several crouching figures picked their way toward the wagons. He could tell by their movement and their hats, these were not Lakota, but white men. The caps told these were soldiers. The invaders circled the wagons and at a signal, they stepped through the circle, rifles at the ready. Suddenly the fire flared, one of the attackers having put more logs on the fire and a man shouted, "Out of your blankets, NOW!"

Sean motioned for Indy to stay and worked his way nearer, watching carefully for any lagging men, and from behind one of the trees nearer the river, he could see what was happening. He immediately recognized Captain Steele and he could hear the man making his demands. "Alright, stand up with your hands on your head! Sergeant, get their rifles!"

"We ain't got no rifles! That scout took 'em!" whined Podunk.

"What? Whaddaya mean you don't have rifles?" demanded the captain.

Podunk sniveled again, "That scout from your fort done took 'em when he made us turn around!"

"Where is he?" ordered the captain.

"I dunno, he left earlier, when we tried to get our rifles back."

The captain watched as several of the teamsters nodded their heads in agreement. "We're takin' the wagons for the Confederacy!" he ordered again.

"The whaaat?"

Before the captain could answer, a voice came from atop one of the wagons. Charlie Canterbury had been aroused by the ruckus and now leaned over the high side, "You can't take these wagons! They don't belong to the army!"

"I'm taking them in the name of the Southern Confederacy! You, climb down outta there!" he ordered.

"There's another man here that's hurt purty bad, he'll need help," answered Charlie.

The captain motioned for two of the teamsters to help Charlie and Whiskers from the wagon. Once the teamsters and roustabouts were gathered, the captain explained, "Your other wagons aren't too far back on the trail so you can join them when they come thisaway." He pointed to the uninjured men, "You men catch up the mules and get 'em hooked up. We're pullin' out right away." He looked around, pointed at three of the men, "You three, you're up on top. You'll be showin' my men how to drive, then you'll be freed to go your own way."

Sean quietly moved back to his camp to be greeted by Fox and Indy. He began to explain what was happening, "There's too many of 'em and they're all around the wagons." He sat down on the log by the grey coals, "Your people ain't gonna be too happy 'bout this. And if they're doin' what I asked Twiss to have 'em do, they're probably close enough to see them pull out with the wagons." He shook his head as he thought about this change of circumstance and he knew it did not bode well for the soldiers.

ONCE THE WAGONS WERE GONE, Sean walked into the camp of the teamsters and was greeted by grumbles and complaints. "If we'd had our rifles, we coulda fought 'em off!" complained Whiskers.

"They snuck in here and had the drop on you and you couldn't stop 'em if you had your rifles!" answered Sean. The men knew he was right but that didn't make their situation any better.

"Wal, then get 'em for us and we'll go after 'em."

Sean chuckled, shaking his head, "So, if you had your rifles, you could chase 'em down on foot? I'd like to see that. So, since your rifles are in those wagons, why don't you just take off after 'em?" said Sean, waving toward the disappearing wagons.

"You mean our rifles were in the wagons all this time?" asked Charlie.

"You were sleepin' on 'em, Charlie," explained Sean. Moans and groans answered Sean's comment as he looked around the group. He added, "You're prob'ly purty lucky, 'cause I'm sure the Lakota already know the wagons are headed down the trail and they'll be after 'em.

I don't think those few soldiers will be able to keep those wagons from ten times that many mad Lakota!" The men looked to one another, considering what Sean had explained.

"Maybe you're right," mumbled Charlie Canterbury.

CHAPTER THIRTY-ONE
ATTACK

THE LOW-LYING BAND OF CLOUDS THAT NESTLED ON THE eastern horizon provided a palette for the lazy sun to show-off with a brilliant gold that was almost blinding to the freighters as they followed the Oregon Trail east. The grey skies of early morning had given them ample light to push a little further, but the mules were dragging their hooves after the long night's travel. Slim had been the first chosen to drive and he hollered at the captain up ahead, "Cap'n! We need to rest these mules! They're 'bout to give out!"

Sergeant O'Reilly was just returning from a forward scout and Steele asked, "Find a place to give these mules a blow?"

The Sergeant twisted in his new army-issued McClellan saddle and pointed, "There! Just past those bluffs! There's a good stretch of grass and a sandy shore so they can water."

"Lead out!" commanded the captain. Then he reined

around to ride back by the freighters, "Follow the sergeant there, we'll take a rest an' have some coffee. Show your man there about unhitching an' watering the mules."

Slim looked at the greenhorn recruit, "Think you can handle 'em, boy?"

Although the recruit was about half the size of the monstrous Slim, he declared, "Anything you can do, I can do!"

Slim chuckled and answered, "Doubt it! But at least yore game, I'll give ya' that!"

The North Platte was not large by any measure, but like any force of water as it pushes its way to some distant destination, it will choose its own course. And when the irresistible force of spring runoff is added, any river carrying that much water will go wherever it wants to, often leaving behind a twisting riverbed with sand, sediment, and seed to quickly be populated with greenery. Now, that wide former riverbed offered graze for the animals as they walked into the belly-deep grass. Cook-fires blossomed and coffee pots danced for an anxious group of new Confederate hopefuls. The captain and the two sergeants sat on a pair of logs, as they considered their location and destination.

"It's gonna be a long haul and we'll be movin' slower with these wagons!" declared O'Reilly.

"Yeah, but those wagons'll give extra cover when we camp at night, at least till we get out of Indian country, and those supplies will make the trip a whole lot easier!" answered Sergeant Watkins. "Ain't that right Cap'n?"

"That's right Sergeant, but more than that, those

wagons also have several crates of rifles and powder and lead that could outfit most of a company." He motioned to the other men, "We've got our rifles, but there's gonna be boys that want to fight that won't have anything but squirrel rifles at best."

"So, what route're we takin' Cap'n?" asked O'Reilly, scooting closer to look at the maps that lay before the officer.

———

WHEN THE GOLD lay on the eastern horizon, Sean and Fox neared the camp of the wagons and Bucky. Once the loaded wagons were taken, sleep was elusive, and the pair mounted up to find their friend and the returning wagons that were to meet up with those of the other teamsters. Sean reined up on a slight knoll to look the camp over before approaching. They had chosen well. With a wide bend of the river, the peninsula in the middle, offered cover both with the water and the young cottonwoods, leaving only the open end of the horseshoe to defend. The wagons were arrayed in a protective circle, with the animals tethered within. For any attacking band, the appearance of the group with the many tall wagons, was deceiving as to the number of defenders. Sean looked to Fox and pointed with his chin, "Guess we better go tell 'em. Bucky ain't gonna be none too happy, that's for sure."

They rode toward the camp, but before Sean could call out, he saw the familiar figure of Bucky with his tall frame, broad chest, and mass of whiskers. The big man waved them in and welcomed them with, "Got some coffee on, come an' sit!"

Sean looked at the man, leaned forward on his pommel, "You might not want me drinkin' your coffee after what I got to tell ya'," drawled Sean.

"Ah, come on. Cain't be that bad. Now climb on down." He looked to Fox and said, "'Sides, your woman looks like she could use a cup, even if you don't!"

As they sat and nursed their coffee, others joined the circle to hear the news. As he told about confronting the men and taking their rifles, Bucky interrupted, "You an' the woman here took that whole bunch, all by your own selves?"

"Well, they had tied one on the night before and weren't none of 'em feelin' too good."

Bucky grabbed up a stick and threw it back to the ground, "So help me, I'll wring that Charlie Canterbury's neck!" he growled.

"I already done that," said Sean softly, grinning.

Bucky looked at him, "You? You took Charlie?!"

"Yeah, but that's not the worst of it," continued Sean and began telling about Captain Steele and his Confederate recruits taking the wagons.

"Consarn it! I figgered you'd try to stop 'em, but I had to let 'em try. After all, I have a contract with Harris and Lafferty and it's their goods, but the Captain? I thought he was a decent sort?!"

"He still is, just on the other side. He coulda just shot all your men, but he didn't. He only took three of 'em to teach his men how to handle those teams, but he left the others for you to pick up on your way through."

Bucky looked at Sean, thought a moment, "That might not be the worst of it. Yestiddy one of my outriders spotted a bunch o' Injuns, Sioux prob'ly, movin' parallel to the trail, headin' thataway," he pointed downstream.

"How many?"

"He guessed at least fifty, prob'ly more. All fightin' men."

"They're Lakota alright. They didn't really trust me to get the wagons back but agreed to give me some time to try." He looked to Bucky, "Think your men'll have sense enough to keep their heads down?"

"Yeah, they will, 'sides, them Injuns are farther out in the flats away from the river. My outrider had to use his telescope to get a good look. An' since they ain't got no wagons, they probably won't even interest them Injuns."

———

"SERGEANT! BREAK OUT A BOX O' that hardtack for the men," ordered the captain.

"You mean some o' them worm castles?" chuckled the sergeant, knowing the men would eat them, but also gripe about them all the while. "Course, some of 'em call 'em dog biscuits and others are callin' 'em belly bombs!" he laughed as he walked to the back of their supply wagon. When he carried the box toward the fire for the waiting men, each man grumbled, but none refused his handful of hardtack. Most would dunk their crackers in their coffee to make it easier on their teeth and gums, as the staple of soldiers and sailors was also known as molar breakers.

He sat the box between him and the captain and both picked at the remains, also choosing to dunk the staple in their coffee. "It's a darn shame, we gotta dunk 'em to be able to eat 'em but then it ruins the coffee!" grumbled O'Reilly.

The captain chuckled at his non-comm, "Sergeant, I'm thinkin' it's gonna get a lot worse before it gets any better. There might come a time in this war that you'll look back on this day and wish you had a box of these by your side."

"If it comes to that, Cap'n, I might have to desert both armies and go back home. Mebbe find me a woman that can cook real biscuits."

"I already have a woman that can cook the best biscuits you ever tasted! She's waitin' for me in Shenandoah," said the Captain, somewhat wistfully as he thought about the blonde-haired beauty that waited.

The two men leaned back against the freight wagon, staring at the small fire where the coffee pot sat rattling its lid. The wagons had been arrayed in a slight arc to serve as a barrier to keep the mules contained as they ate their fill. The men had gathered around a pair of campfires, talking and putting away the hardtack and coffee. One of the teamsters had climbed back atop his wagon to retrieve his coffee cup and hollered out, "Injuns!" as he jumped to the ground. When his feet hit the ground, he was peppered with questions, but he hollered back, "Hunnerts of 'em, yonder!" pointing to the slight slope and the wide flats.

The soldiers scattered, grabbing their rifles and finding cover. The captain shouted orders, "Take cover! Hold your fire! Wait for my command!"

The wagons were too tall for the soldiers to shoot over, unless they climbed up to the spring seat, but then they became a prime target for any attackers. Many bellied down under the wagon box, using the spokes of the wheels for cover, while others took to one end or the other, preferring to stand to shoot.

The Captain and Sergeant O'Reilly were at one space between two wagons and were both astounded to see the line of Lakota spread out and sitting their mounts at least three hundred yards away. The obvious leader was in the center of the line of what Steele estimated as forty warriors. He mumbled, "Well, at least it ain't hundreds!"

"What's that Cap'n? asked O'Reilly.

"I said that doesn't look like hundreds."

"No, but it's a sight more'n we have," answered the Sergeant, holding his rifle with white-knuckled paws.

"But we have Springfields. Most of the men can shoot two, three times a minute, and I'm thinkin' that kinda evens the odds."

"Yeah," grumbled O'Reilly, "But that's on the rifle range shootin' at targets. Most o' those young recruits will prob'ly shoot once an' wet their pants!"

Both the Captain and Sergeant had ridden with General Harney at Ash Hollow and other skirmishes and were confident they could defend themselves here, but the experienced Sergeant knew his men and could easily tell who would stand and fight and who would cower in fear. The captain looked at the man, "You don't think any'll run, do ya'?"

"They won't run far, that's for sure. But if any of 'em tries, I think the others'll keep 'em fightin'."

It was the common practice for the Lakota to send in a wave of warriors to draw the first fire, and the second wave would charge before the defenders had time to reload. But these Lakota had not been confronted with the new Spring-field rifles. With the paper-patch bullets and percussion caps, the Springfield gave the soldiers the ability to fire more often and reload more quickly. As the Captain watched, the leader of the Lakota, Standing Elk, raised his rifle high and shouted. The first wave of about fifteen warriors kicked their horses to a run and started for the wagons.

Captain Steele shouted, "Wait . . . wait . . . fire!" The barrage of rifle shots sounded almost as one; the massive explosion and belched cloud of smoke assailed the attack-ers. A handful of the Indians were knocked from their mounts, two other horses tumbled end over end, throwing their riders. But before the smoke lifted, the remainder of the Lakota were screaming their war cries as they charged into the melee. Rifles from both sides barked and sent their leaden death through the smoky cloud that dimmed everyone's view and limited their marksmanship.

Two soldiers had exposed themselves between the wagons and both lay on their backs, bleeding. One from a bullet hole in his neck, the other impaled with two arrows in his chest. As the soldiers struggled to reload, the warriors charged again, arrows raining down on the soldiers and smoke from both the soldiers' and the Lakota rifles so thick it was hard to see and difficult to breathe. A groan from under the wagon by the Captain told of another wounded soldier. Sergeant O'Reilly had dropped his rifle and was hammering away with his sidearm, when a well-placed lance buried itself in his chest, knocking him backwards to the ground, both hands on the shaft, wide eyes looking to the Captain, and blood coming from his mouth. In an instant, his hands fell to his side and his eyes stared, unseeing.

A short pause in the fighting allowed the cloud of smoke to lift enough to see the Lakota had pulled back to their line, facing the wagons, waiting to charge again. Suddenly a hail of arrows came from behind the barrier of wagons and the Captain turned to see another forty or more Lakota, on foot, charging toward the surprised men. But Steele didn't see the arrow that plowed into his throat and choked the life from him.

The screams and war cries from the band led by Red Cloud told Standing Elk of their attack and he waved his warriors to again charge. Although the battle raged incessantly, for what seemed like hours, the entire conflict had taken less than fifteen minutes and every blue clad soldier was dead. One of the teamsters lay with the soldiers, but two, Slim and O'Malley, had been checking on the mules when the attack came, and they quickly took cover. But when they thought it was all over and they stepped from their cover, they were quickly captured and taken to Red Cloud.

The warriors had busied themselves taking scalps and plunder from the bodies, with much shouting and dancing around, but Red Cloud stood complacently beside Standing Elk as they waited for the celebration to subside. Another war leader stood at their side, *Tȟašúŋke Kȟokíphapi,* They-Fear-Even-His-Horse, and when the two captive teamsters were brought before them, he asked, "You drive wagons?"

"Yeah, both of us," declared Slim, motioning to himself and O'Malley.

"Good. You drive," ordered the war leader. "Get

mules," he commanded as he nodded to the many animals still grazing.

"Sure, sure," answered Slim, and started to the trees where the harness hung. He looked to O'Malley and hissed, "Hurry up, don't wanna make 'em wanna kill us too!"

CHAPTER THIRTY-TWO
PACT

"So, what'chu think they'll do?" asked Bucky, looking to Sean and Fox.

Sean turned to look at Fox then back to Bucky, "I don't think they'll let those wagons get away. Anybody that's on 'em oughta be makin' peace with their maker cuz the Lakota are determined to never be cheated again! The younger leaders have been leanin' towards all-out war against all the whites for some time now, and this could just push 'em that way!"

"Yeah, but there was only 'bout five hunnert warriors round the fort. The army can put more'n that in the field," exclaimed a frustrated Bucky.

"Bucky, you're in their territory. What you saw was nothin', only 'bout three bands of the Lakota. There's probably ten times that many in all their territory. And add into that all the Cheyenne, Arapaho and others that would join them against the whites," he shook his head at the thought of the destruction and death that would come if all the tribes joined together.

"Yuh think we oughta go see if we can help them sojers?" asked Bucky, wondering.

"You said your outrider saw what he thought was maybe fifty warriors?"

"That's right, fifty."

"If he saw fifty, there were probably more'n a hundred." He looked around the camp, "And you've got what, thirty at most? And the other camp, maybe ten. And you wanna take that many, drivin' these big wagons or ridin' mules, against more'n a hundred stompin' mad, proven warriors?"

"Nah, you're right. Ain't no sense in doin' that." He tramped around for a moment, looked at Sean, "But I'm responsible fer them wagons!" he declared, stomping his foot and shaking his head.

Sean stood and looked around, thinking about what possibilities remained, rubbing the back of his neck as Fox had seen him do when he was working out a problem. He looked to Fox and asked, "Will they want to keep the wagons and mules?"

She thought about what he said and with her head cocked a little to the side, she grinned, "There are some that like mule meat, but not many. If they are hungry, they may take some. But they do not need the big wagons."

Sean looked to Bucky who turned back, grinning, "That herd of beef came in after you left. They should be happy with them. Maybe they'll leave my mules alone!" He scowled, "Who would wanna eat mules anyway? Ain't they kinda tough?"

Sean chuckled, remembering what his pa said about the expedition with Fremont and how all the men gladly ate mule rather than starve. He said, "You ain't never been hungry enough, have you?" motioning to the big belly on the man.

Bucky laughed, putting his hands to his belly, "Reckon not, ain't missed too many meals, that's for sure!" He sat down, looked up to Sean, "But, what're we gonna do?"

Sean sat down next to the big man, dwarfed in his shadow, and with a hand on Bucky's shoulder, "The Lakota will be bringin' them wagons back through here," nodding toward the trail that paralleled the river, "and maybe we," motioning toward Fox, "can talk to 'em. If we can make 'em understand that you didn't have anything to do with what went on, then maybe you can follow 'em back to the fort and get your wagons after they empty 'em."

"What about muh men, didn't you say the sojers took three of 'em?"

"They did. The big guy I think they call Slim, 'nother fella with a shock of wavy red hair, and one that was bald 'cepin' for a ring of hair just above his ears."

"Yeah, that'd be Slim, as you said, an' O'Malley and Friar, they called him that cuz somebody had read them ol' books 'bout the brown robes o'er in England what shaved their heads." He chuckled, remembering each one, then sobered as he looked to Sean, "You don't suppose . . ." he started, but Sean was shaking his head. Bucky dropped his eyes, "They was good men, too."

Sean considered the men, also remembering. He also thought about what some of the native people do to those that are their enemies like he had described to the other teamsters. He hoped that didn't happen to Bucky's friends, knowing the best he could hope for was a quick and merciful death for all of them. He had paced around a bit, thinking, and sat back down next to Bucky. "The way I figger, the earliest they could get back by here would be toward dark, but they might take longer an' we won't see 'em till sometime tomorrow. Might be a good time for your men to stay busy with harness and wagon repair or somethin' to keep their minds off things. But whatever they do, have 'em keep their rifles handy! Once some o' them young bucks get a taste of blood an' such, they can be hard to hold back."

THE WESTERN HORIZON cradled the golden orb as swords of white lanced the remaining blue of the heavens. Random clouds caught and held shades of orange and gold appearing to be playful cherubs that had waded in golden puddles. Sean and Fox sat together on a wide, flat sandstone, feet dangling over the side, each quietly pondering what was to come. Fox turned her head at a slight angle, looked to Sean out of the corner of her eye and asked, "Do you want me with you when you talk to Standing Elk?"

Sean frowned, "How do you know it will be Standing Elk leading them?"

"Either Standing Elk or Red Cloud will be leading. That is the way of the people. It must be a strong war leader for this, and they are the most respected of those that were by the fort."

Sean nodded his head in understanding, "Yes, I want you with me. I'm tolerable with the language, but you are a warrior of the people and they have to listen to you!"

She smiled, leaned toward him, "Is that the only reason, boyfriend?"

He put an arm around her, but she felt him stiffen as he looked to the east at the approaching wagons. "They're coming. We need to meet 'em 'fore they see these other wagons."

THE WAR LEADERS rode at the front of the wagons and warriors, Standing Elk and Red Cloud together, followed by Touch the Clouds and They Fear Even His Horse. Warriors were strung out beside the wagons with Slim driving the first pair, O'Malley the second, and two warriors leading the mules of the third set. The smaller supply wagon of the soldiers was driven by a warrior. Sean and Fox waited, sitting horseback in the middle of the trail. As the war leaders neared, Sean held his hand up in both a greeting and a sign for them to stop. When the procession came to a standstill, Sean and Fox rode side by side to face the war leaders.

"A'ho! Bear Chaser and White Fox. Why are you here?" spoke Standing Elk. Red Cloud sat stoically as Touch the Clouds and Horse came alongside.

Sean had scanned what he could see of the wagons and was surprised to see Slim atop the first one. "The leader of the wagons, a man named Bucky, would like to get his wagons back."

The statement surprised the chiefs and they looked around, as if they expected to see many soldiers or armed men ready to take the wagons by force and battle. Seeing none, Standing Elk frowned, "I do not understand. We know you had taken the wagons and were bringing them back to the fort, but the bluecoats took them and were leaving. Now you ask for them back?"

"No, the supplies in the wagons are yours as they should be. But you have no need for the wagons. The man that led the others to bring all these supplies to your people, he wants the wagons and the mules so he can return and bring more supplies to your people."

"He did not surrender all the supplies before, and his men took the wagons with the rifles and powder. Now they will take no more!" declared Red Cloud.

"This man was not with those that stole the wagons. He and the others are in a camp waiting for your word," explained Fox.

Standing Elk looked at the woman, back to Sean, then turned to the other war leaders. Seeing no objection from them, he looked back to Sean, "We will take the wagons to the fort. When they are empty, this man can have the wagons and mules for ten horses!"

Sean was surprised, but pleased. Ten horses were a lot cheaper than trying to take the wagons by force, wagons that he didn't really think they would get at any price. He extended his arm towards Standing Elk and moved closer, "Agreed!" The two men clasped forearms and nodded their heads in agreement to part, but Sean remembered the two teamsters. "The two white men that are driving, did they kill any Lakota?"

Red Cloud laughed, "They were hiding in the trees when we fought. They were taken after the battle."

"They are needed to drive the wagons back," explained Sean.

Horse spoke up, "I have claimed their scalps! The one with fire shall decorate my lance!" he declared.

Sean looked at him and said, "There is no honor in taking a captive's scalp." When Horse scowled, Sean looked to Standing Elk. "Is this the kind of warrior you lead, one who takes a scalp from a captive. I see no fresh scalps on his lance, did he not fight with you?"

Sean saw a grin tug at the corner of the older chief's mouth as he recognized what Sean was doing and Standing Elk looked to Horse, "Will you take five horses for the scalps of the captives?"

Horse knew he had to save face and pulled his horse back and grunted to Standing Elk, "Done!"

Sean nodded as he and Fox reined aside so the group could move further to find a camp before total dark. Fox smiled at her man and the duo pointed their horses to the camp by the river. She was proud of her man and pleased they could tell the big friend he could have his wagons and men.

CHAPTER THIRTY-THREE
REPARATIONS

"Ten horses!? Where'm I gonna get ten horses?" exclaimed Bucky, hands out from his sides as he glared at Sean.

"Well, actually, more like fifteen!"

"Fifteen? Why fifteen?"

"Ten for the wagons, five for your men," stated Sean, soberly. This was the first Bucky heard about his men even being alive.

"What men?" he asked, having lowered his voice as his curiosity raised.

"Slim and O'Malley. One of the chiefs had already claimed O'Malley's red scalp, but he said he'd let you have 'em for five horses."

"Hummph," he grunted, trying to look disgusted but having a hard time keeping his expression grim with the good news. "Ain't sure they're worth five horses," he grumbled. He looked up at Sean, "They're alive huh? So, where'm I gonna get fifteen horses?"

"Oh, I'm sure you can trade some of the Lakota out of

that many horses. You get some trade goods from Fort Bernard on your way through, probably some rifles for the men and some pots for the women, a few blankets, and a little dickering, you can prob'ly get enough."

SEAN, Fox, Bucky, and three other teamsters rode into the fort late in the afternoon. Fox said her goodbye to Sean as she was bound to visit her family. Two pack-mules were laden with goods picked up at Fort Bernard and all the animals were tethered in front of the Sutler's. Sean started for the commandant's office while Bucky and his men went to the sutler's for additional goods and hoping he could steer them to someone with horses to trade.

"MR. SAINT! I am mighty glad to see you. What can you tell me about the other freighters?" He had extended his hand to greet Sean and now sat back in the chair behind the desk.

"I see you've settled in to the commandant's job," observed Sean.

"Well, I am the ranking officer, actually, I'm the only officer since Steele left." The Lieutenant saw a somber expression paint Sean's face and he leaned forward, "What is it?"

Sean began to explain all the happenings of the last few days and how the Captain had taken the supply freighters from the teamsters. "When he commandeered the wagons, he said he was taking them in the name of the Southern Confederacy. They had no intention of bringing them back to the fort and the Lakota."

The Lieutenant leaned back, put his hands together, finger tips touching and explained, "Yeah, he said they were going to fight for the Confederacy. I told him I didn't relish the idea of being on opposite sides and maybe shooting at each other." He shook his head as he remembered their conversation. "I hated to see 'em do it but couldn't stop him. He signed out a bunch of supplies and a wagon. There was a dozen that deserted with him, two sergeants and the rest were buck privates and recruits. Kinda leaves us short-handed, but I haven't notified headquarters yet. Thought I'd give 'em a day or two to maybe change their mind." The Lieutenant spoke wistfully and hopefully, turning to look out the window to take his gaze from Sean.

Sean paused a moment, then spoke softly, "You can notify your headquarters now. They won't be coming back."

The Lieutenant swiveled the chair around to face Sean, eyebrows lifted and looking wide-eyed at the man before him.

Sean explained, "They're all dead. The Lakota refused to let them take the supplies, rifles and such, that were promised to them. The Captain didn't want to give 'em up. So, the Confederacy will have to do without 'em."

The Lieutenant leaned forward, "Then we'll have to make those Indians pay!"

Sean slowly shook his head as he looked down and back up to the officer, "Couple things you might wanna think about 'fore you try that Lieutenant. First off, you've got less than a hundred men here, not half of 'em battle proven, and you would be goin' against about five hundred warriors. Then you need to consider the men that were killed were deserters. Now, from what I know about your regulations, a deserter could get shot anyway. And if you met each other a few months from now, you might have been the one to shoot the captain your own self. So, you ready to go risk the lives of all your men and your own scalp just to try to prove a point?"

The uniformed officer leaned back, crossed his arms across his chest and looked at Sean. Although the Lieutenant was eight or ten years older and had been a career Army officer for that same number of years, he realized the young man before him had greater wisdom than his years. He considered the advice for a few moments then asked, "What do you suggest?"

"Most of these folks'll be leaving soon, now that they have their supplies, so I think the best thing for ever'body would be for you to stay right here inside this fort. Most of the Lakota have a certain respect for this place and for most of the soldiers, but after their little fight with Captain Steele, any provocation on your part might just set off a powder keg and be more trouble than anybody wants. I've talked to some of the chiefs and they'll let the teamsters take the wagons back, as long as Bucky can get enough horses together, and they'll leave for their summer camp and hunting territory."

The Lieutenant shook his head at the mention of territory, "Yeah, I found some orders that General Harney left, and we're supposed to be keeping order between the tribes and making sure they're stayin' in their own territories. So, you tell me how we're supposed to do that with less than a hundred men?"

Sean chuckled, "That would be a job for a couple of regiments, not your handful. And the territories you mention, by the way, ain't nuthin' like the maps you have. The Lakota have taken back most of the territory from the Crow and they're still fightin' over it from time to time. And the Assiniboine and Arikara have also been pushed back by the Lakota."

"Sounds like the Lakota are fighting everybody around, including us!" He leaned forward on the desk, "Are you going to still scout for the fort?"

"I've done all I can for now. I never thought I'd hafta try to be a go-between the Lakota people, the Army, and the government as well. So, I'm takin' some time off. I'll be at my cabin by South Pass settlin' in with my new wife!"

"Wife? You mean that Lakota woman that's been with you?"

"Ummhumm, I think her mama's puttin' together some kind of 'joinin' ceremony, what we'd call a wedding."

"South Pass? That's where your cabin is? But isn't that Arapaho country?"

"That's right."

The Lieutenant grinned and shook his head, "Talk about gumption. Taking a Lakota woman into Arapaho country and making a home."

SEAN FOUND Bucky waiting by the horses, "Looks like we're gonna be set! The Sutler had 'nuff horses he'd traded from the Injuns and we gave him the trade goods and a little to boot. So, can you let that chief know we can make the deal an' get muh wagons back?"

Sean grinned at the big man, "Sure can, Bucky. Be glad

to. You hang around here and I'll send one of 'em over to get you so you can settle up."

"Are we gonna see ya' 'fore we leave?" asked the big man.

Sean chuckled, "Don't think so. I got a wedding to get ready for!"

"A wedding?! So, you're gonna do it after all?"

"Yup."

"Well congratulations boy! I'm mighty happy fer ya'. Say, next time you see yore pa, be sure to tell him I said Howdy. Would'ja do that fer me?"

"Of course, Bucky." Sean extended his hand, but Bucky slapped it away and wrapped the young man in a bear hug, picking him up off the ground and swinging his around as he roared like a bear. When he dropped him to the ground, he looked soberly at Sean and said, "You've been a good friend Sean. I'll never forget it!"

"And you as well, Bucky." He started away, turned around and said, "Keep your topknot on!" and walked through the gate of the fort, leading Dusty and the dapple grey with Indy trotting beside him.

CHAPTER THIRTY-FOUR
PREPARATIONS

It was a restless night for Sean. Often tossing and turning, getting tangled in his blankets, frustrated as he looked around. Even Indy was often up and pacing, looking, watching. Sean would doze, awaken and look to the horses, knowing Fox's paint was missing, roll to his side with his back to the animals, and frustrated all the more when he heard the soft padding of Indy's paws as he searched for the woman. He would pinch his eyes closed, try to shut out the night sounds, but the memories of their few weeks together would rush in and he would re-live every day, every conversation, every moment that brought smiles and happiness to his life.

He finally rolled to his back, put his clasped hands behind his head and looked to the star filled sky thinking about what was to come. He looked at the Milky Way arching over the black velvet and thought of *Wanagi Tacanku* the name given the Milky Way by the people of the Lakota. He remembered Fox telling him the Wicasa Wakan or Holy Man had explained that one of the four souls of each person would travel the road beyond to meet with an old woman where the soul is examined to determine its ultimate destination, either the spirit world or to return to be reborn to try again to live in harmony.

He searched the night sky for the north star, starting with the Orion constellation, or as the people called it, the Great Bear. When he found the north star, he was reminded of the many times he traveled by night, much like his father, with only that star to guide him. But he also was reminded of the Creator of all that always goes with him, even when the star was not visible. He smiled at the comfort of knowing the God of all creation as his personal Savior. He looked to the moon, slowly waxing towards full, and as it hung suspended upon nothing nearing the western horizon, he realized morning was fast approaching.

He rolled from his blankets, stirred the coals and added a few sticks. He stood and stretched before starting the coffee. Indy came to his side, demanding some attention and Sean sat on the log, his hand on the scruff of the wolf's neck, "Well, Indy, today's the day. No more lonely nights like this one, we're gonna be a family! The only thing I'm wonderin' is who's gonna get more attention, you or me?" The wolf seemed to understand and smiled as he lifted his eyes to Sean as of to emphasize what was the obvious, that Indy would definitely get more attention.

He poured himself a cup of coffee, picked up his Bible, and walked to the edge of the river to seat himself at the base of a big cottonwood and face the rising sun. He had a heart-to-heart talk with his Lord, emptying himself of doubt and weight of sin, sharing every concern and hope and need, and expressing his love and worship for his God. As the rising sun gave color to the east and light to see, Sean turned the pages of his Bible to the place he stopped reading the day before and began to read and refresh his Spirit with the Word. He was reading in the first chapter of Romans, verse 12, *That is, that I may be comforted together with you by the mutual faith both of you and me.* He smiled, thinking of the times spent with Fox and that they would be together and be comforted together. He continued to the next verse, *Now I would not have you ignorant brethren,* and he frowned as he looked again at those words. But a soft voice interrupted his thoughts.

"Hello, my boyfriend."

He smiled and turned to see Fox standing with one hand on the rough bark of the cottonwood and smiling down on him. The color of the sunrise reflected on her face and her eyes twinkled as she looked at him. He lifted a hand to bid her sit with him. She leaned her head on his shoulder as she slipped her hand through the crook of his arm. He chuckled, "I sure am glad to see you! I was just reading, and it said, *I would not have you ignorant brethren,* and my first thought was that you wouldn't have this ignorant man," pointing at his chest, "but you came just in time!"

She frowned and asked, "You thought your God did not want me to be with you?"

"No, no, I was reading it wrong. I thought it was saying that you wouldn't want me!"

"Oh, but I do!" she pouted.

"And I want you too," he declared.

She leaned back and turned to look directly at him to

ask, "I want to know more about your God. You say you know for sure you will be in His Heaven, how?"

He smiled and looked down at his Bible. He flipped through a few pages and began to explain, "God loves us unconditionally, but He hates sin, or wrongdoing." He told how everyone sins and there is a penalty for that sin, "That penalty is death and hell forever. But He doesn't want us to go there, so He sent His son, Jesus, to pay that penalty for us, which He did when He died on the cross."

Fox asked, "What is the cross?"

"That's the way the rulers or chiefs of the time tortured and killed their enemies."

"Oh," and nodded her head for him to continue.

"So, when He died, his death bought us a gift, the gift of eternal life or . . ." and he thought of how to explain it simply. "It's like the gift of getting to spend all eternity in His Heaven."

Fox smiled and nodded, understanding.

"But like any gift, we have to accept it."

"How?" she asked simply

"By prayer, we simply ask Him to forgive us of our sins or wrongdoing and ask Him for the gift Jesus bought when he died for us."

"So, we have to have *Wicasa Wakan* to pray for us and offer the prayers with the smoke of the pipe?"

Sean smiled, "No, we can do that ourselves. Like when I come in the morning and talk with God. That's prayer or talking with Him. So, all we do is pray, or talk to Him, and ask for that gift."

"We don't need to smoke the pipe to offer the prayers?"

"No."

"And we don't need the Holy Man, *Wicasa Wakan*, to pray for us?"

"No, see when Jesus died, He made the way for each one to go directly to God with our prayers."

"I like that! Can we do that now?"

"Of course. It's easy. I tell you what, I'll pray, and you can say the same prayer after me. But only if you really mean it," and he pointed to her heart, "here."

She nodded her head enthusiastically, smiling, and listened as Sean began, "Our Father, . . ." and continued to ask forgiveness and to ask for the gift of eternal life with Christ coming to live within. Fox repeated every phrase exactly and when Sean said 'Amen," she did the same, only a little louder and much more excitedly. She clapped her hands and said, "Now I know your God!"

"No, now you know *our* God!"

"Yes. That makes me very happy!" she declared. She stood and looked down at Sean, "A man will come for you. You will go to the lodge of Buffalo Walking, our *Wicasa Wakan* and he will tell you of our way of joining. My father, Crow Dog, will also be there and two war leaders. You will be told what you are to do. Then you will come to the joining with me!" She clapped her hands giddily and trotted off, leaving Sean staring after her.

SEAN WAS JUST FINISHING his second cup of coffee when Indy jumped to his feet, looking to the crest of the bank, to see a young man approaching.

"I am Running Badger, you are to come with me," the young man stated as if Sean had no choice. But Sean nodded, threw the dregs of the coffee aside, and dropped the cup and started after the young man. The lodge was painted with several designs and colors that probably had some significance or even message, but Sean didn't understand them. He was directed to enter, and he bent to step into the lodge. A small fire burned in the center ring, more for light than warmth, and illuminated the interior. He gave a quick glance that showed many bundles and packages that hung from the poles and were stacked around the edges.

The central figure was obviously the holy man, Buffalo Walking. His headdress was the crest of a buffalo head complete with horns and cape that draped down his back. His braids hung over his shoulders and his countenance was stern. With a quick motion, he told Sean to be seated in front of him. Once seated, Sean looked to the man as he offered the pipe to the four directions, Father Sky and Mother Earth, took a deep draught and passed it to the man on his left. Crow Dog repeated the motions and passed the pipe to Red Cloud who in turn passed it to Sean. Sean did the same, passing the pipe to Little Thunder who passed to Standing Elk and then to Buffalo Walking.

The holy man looked to Sean, "We have offered our prayers to Wakan Tanka and now we are to teach you of our people and your duty as a man that is joined to a woman of the Lakota." Sean nodded and listened as each man took his turn to give Sean counsel as to the people and for him as a man. He heard of the responsibility to provide for and protect those of his lodge and of the extended family that included the people. His duties as a father not just to those of his lodge but to those of other families were also explained. As the counsel completed the circle, he nodded his understanding. Buffalo Walking handed him a bundle, "You will go and wash. If you want to use a sweat lodge, Crow Dog will show you to one. You will put on those skins and return for the joining." The holy man waved his scepter which was a hawk's wing adorned with beads and fringe and sent Sean from the lodge.

He returned to his camp, stripped and waded into the backwater of the river that he had used before to bathe, and scrubbed down with a coarse bar of lye soap. After drying off, he sat on the grass and opened the bundle. At his first sight of the attire, he paused to look. He reached to touch the soft white buckskin and slowly ran his fingers over the beading that covered a wideband over the shoulders and down on the yoke. The buckskin of the yoke was of a blue-green and the contrasting bright colors of white and yellow beads accented the shoulders and chest. He slipped on the leggings whose only adornment was the long braid that hung the length of the leg on each side. The rest of the tunic was of white buckskin like the leggings and the yoke and sleeves were adorned with long fringe. But this fringe was different with each strip twisted tightly and hanging separately with tufts of rabbit fur at the end of every tenth fringe. The fringe that hung from the yoke had alternating strips of blue-green and white, accenting the separate colors of the yoke and the rest of the tunic. The long tail of the tunic was raw and almost appeared as ragged, but the irregular edge was an accent rather than a distraction. Once dressed, Sean ran his hands over the soft buckskin thinking he had never felt leather so smooth and soft. He put on the matching moccasins that had beading exactly like that at his shoulders. The long fringe of the leggings dangled to the ground but showed a certain elegance.

He smiled, walked to the edge of the water to see his reflection in the backwater pool, and chuckled at himself. He ran his fingers through his hair then started back to the lodge of Buffalo Running for any other preparations for the joining.

CHAPTER THIRTY-FIVE
CHANGE

SEAN, TRAILED BY INDY, WALKED BEHIND BUFFALO Walking as he led toward the central compound of the village. Most of the villagers had gathered and stood among the lodges making a large circle. Two young men, carrying a big bundle, followed Sean, and stood behind him and the holy man. Indy lay down beside Sean, eyes alert and mouth open, tongue lolling, looking as if he was smiling.

Behind the circle, a low rhythmic beat of a drum began, and the people parted. From a far lodge came a procession of women led by Runs in Water, Crow Dog's woman and Fox's Lakota mother. Other grey-haired women followed and as they came to the circle, each stepped to the side to reveal Fox. Sean caught his breath when he first saw her. She seemed to glow in her bright white fringed dress. A beaded sash draped over one shoulder and across to her opposite hip, ending with long fringe down her leg. The beads on the drape were mostly shades of red, orange and yellow in an intriguing design.

Across her shoulders and down the yoke was a wide pattern of blue and white beads that looked as if waves of crystalline water washed over her neck and shoulders. A row of tiny metal bells hung from short fringe across her chest and ivory elk teeth adorned the seam of her sleeves. Fringe came from the point of her shoulders and cascaded down her arms, each piece with tufts of fur at the end.

Fox's hair hung in loose braids over her shoulders, interwoven with bits of white fur. An intricate beaded blue and white necklace choker trailing long strings of beads decorated her throat and neck. A tuft of white fur at the back of her head held two banded feathers. In her hands she held a white wing with a beaded holder. With her eyes downcast, Fox slowly walked to Sean's side, prompting Indy to rise-up and watch as she neared. As soon as Fox stopped, Indy dropped to his belly, staying near protectively.

Buffalo Running stepped before them, the pipe cradled in his arm. He lifted the pipe to his lips, took a deep puff and as he released the smoke, he used his free hand with the wing, to wave the smoke over the couple. After a moment, he motioned to the two young men to come forward and open the buffalo robe. Painted on the hide was a scene of a buffalo hunt with a white buffalo in the middle of the herd. Buffalo Running began, "Crow Dog tells of their hunt when the people saw the white buffalo. That is a good omen for the people. And it was on that night that the black wolf came to White Fox and saved her from the others. The next day came Bear Chaser bearing the gift of meat for the women of the village. Crow Dog was confused. The white buffalo is a good sign as is *Ptehincalaskawin*, White Buffalo Calf Woman. But *Iktomi*, the trickster, often comes in the form of a wolf. Then this man, Bear Chaser came with gifts. So, Crow Dog waited and watched and determined that this man was the message sent by the white buffalo and now he is to be joined to White Fox and the people."

He motioned for the young men to place the robe over the shoulders of Sean and Fox. The two to be joined held the robe and drew closer beneath. Buffalo Running said simply, "As you are together beneath this robe of blessing, may you be together always." He stepped back and looked to the people, "They are one!" The crowd burst into cheers and shouts and scattered to lay out the feast to celebrate the joining. Sean was startled when the crowd shouted, but the smile on Fox's face told him all was well. He put his hands to her waist and drew her near and the two enjoyed a lingering kiss. When Fox drew back, she looked up to her man and said, "Now, you really are my boyfriend!"

Sean chuckled, hugged her, and with his lips by her ear, "I was always your boyfriend! And now you are my wife!" He leaned back, smiling and kissed her again.

AS THEY SAT TOGETHER, enjoying the feast, many of the people came by, touching their hands on their shoulders and offering best wishes and congratulations in the custom of the people. The feast and dancing lasted most of the afternoon, Sean and Fox participating in most, but soon tiring, they sat back to enjoy the celebration. But as dusk approached, the people slowly made their way to their own lodges to leave the new couple alone. As was the custom of the Lakota, the mother of Fox and her friends had prepared a new lodge for them and it was set off to the side of the village, closer to the river and the trees. Their horses had been tended to by the young men of the village and they were free to spend the time together, Indy standing guard outside the entry flap. As they neared the tipi, Sean grinned and scooped up his new wife, holding her cradled in his arms, "And this is a custom of my people!" He pushed aside the entry flap and stepped in, still holding Fox and as they entered their new home, he kissed her as he held her. With a broad smile, he lowered her feet to the ground and allowed her to stand. Stepping back, he said, "You are the most beautiful bride in the world!"

ALL THE BRULÉ and most of the Oglala were breaking camp, packing everything on travois and packhorses as they prepared to return to their summer encampments to hunt and prepare for the coming winter. Sean had replenished their supplies and added a pair of pack-mules to handle their new hide lodge. With the weight of the buffalo hides, most of the people used a travois to haul the lodge, but Sean preferred to split the bundle and haul only the hides. Where they were bound, he could easily cut the tall lodgepoles for the tipi.

Fox had said her goodbyes and the Brulé started to the north as Sean and Fox bore to the west and the long trek over the Laramie range, the wide basin of the Medicine Bow river, and on to follow the Sweetwater to South Pass. It would be at least a ten-day journey, more likely two weeks, but it would also be a journey of discovery, especially for Fox since she had never been to the Wind River

Mountains and Sean was anxious for her to see their new home.

It was just at a week of travel when they hit the Sweetwater river. Sean took Fox to Independence Rock and they took the time to climb and look at all the names that had been carved into the big rock. They sat down atop the massive stone, enjoying the panorama, as Sean spoke, "I guess they think they've really done sumpin' by makin' it this far. I reckon they're right, seein' how so many don't make it."

"Is it not always so, with all people. When they complete something special, they want to remember that and will make a mark or something. The ancients would carve the stories in stone for their children to see and remember. I have seen many places where these stories are written, much like these," she said as she waved her hand to the names on the rock.

Sean grinned, remembering a time with his father. "I have seen some of those with my pa. We were hunting deer and came across a small canyon with steep red walls and there were all sorts of figures chipped into those stones. Pa tried to read the stories but couldn't quite make 'em out. Some of the figures were men, others you could tell were buffalo or deer or antelope. But some, well, it was hard to tell what they were."

They stood and started off the rock, picking their way carefully on the rough stone. Sean sat down and slid for a ways and turned to catch Fox as she followed. "Careful!" said Sean as they scampered off the big rock.

As they walked to where the horses were tethered,

"Where do they all come from?" asked Fox, having a hard time comprehending so many people from so many places. Some had inscribed the dates and their home state along with their names or initials. Sean had pointed out some recent sign of a passing wagon train when they arrived at the rock.

"Well, from all over. For most of 'em, it takes several months just to make it this far, and it'll take a couple more at least, to get to Oregon or wherever they're goin'. Ya' see, when you go back east, past the big river, there's so many people you can't ride for a day without seein' people, and their farms and homes and cities."

"Will more come?"

Sean chuckled, "Oh yeah. It's not just people from the east. There's folks from across the ocean that come over from those lands by ship. Then they come this way for the land. And it seems like they just keep comin' and comin'. Pa says the day will come when there will be roads ever'where and towns and people and farms. They're puttin' up the telegraph wires, already got 'em at the Fort, and the stagecoach lines are pushin' west. Won't be like it is now, where we can ride for days and not see another person, native or white."

"Can they be stopped?" asked Fox, thinking of her people that were fighting for their lands against the Crow and others. Now it seemed they would have to fight the white man as well.

Sean dropped his eyes, shaking his head, "I'm afraid not. I just hope our children will get to enjoy the wilderness like we do."

Fox smiled at his mention of children. They both mounted up and rode on alongside the Sweetwater. Their trail took them through a narrow cut between two towering rock formations that required them to walk their horses into the small river to pass through. Once on the other side, they took to the grass along the river bank and made their camp.

The third day after climbing Independence Rock, they overtook a long line of white bonneted wagons just making camp beside the Sweetwater near the Sweetwater Rocks, a cluster of large rocky knolls that appeared out of place on the flats by the river. The wagons were camped between the rocks and the river and Sean chose to bypass them by swinging wide of the big rocks. They made about five or six miles more before they stopped for their break and meal.

"I been thinkin' we might go back to travelin' at night. This country is both Crow and Arapaho and Cheyenne, and there's time some of the Ute come this far north. I'd just as soon move on after we have a little rest for the animals and a bite of food for ourselves."

They dismounted and stripped the animals, giving them a chance to roll before Sean rubbed them down with a handful of grass. While he busied himself with the horses, Fox readied the gear and started a cook fire. She walked to Sean's side, "Are there many fish in the river?" she asked, nodding her head toward the stream.

He looked at her grin, head cocked at an angle, and knew what she wanted. "Alright, I'll go see if I can get us a couple trout. Won't take long."

In a short while he returned, holding three nice cutthroat trout. Fox gladly accepted the prize, putting two in the pan and tossing the other to Indy. Sean looked at her, "No wonder that wolf likes you better'n me!

You're gonna make him so lazy he won't hunt for himself!"

As they continued, still traveling by daylight, Sean had noticed and was concerned when he saw a long line of poles carrying a single wire in the direction they were traveling. They had crossed the Sweetwater and followed the trail for three more days when Sean saw a thin line of smoke pointing to the blue sky. With no breeze, the smoke rose unhindered and as they neared, Sean was surprised to see three log cabins next to the trail where another crossing of the river was offered. He reined up and sat staring. "Now when . . ." he started, looked to Fox and said, "those weren't there the last time we came through here!" pointing at the cabins. He looked for a moment longer, saw a couple of people moving between the cabins and gigged Dusty forward.

It was mid-day and Sean had not thought of stopping, but when an odd-looking fella that waddled like a pregnant duck lifted his hand and shouted a greeting, his curiosity got the better of him. They approached and the man said, "Howdy stranger! Won't you an' the missus get down? I've got coffee on an' you're welcome!"

Sean had noticed the poles and wire ended at this cabin and he wondered what that was all about, so he stepped down. The man offered his hand as he said, "I'm Wooster! Used to be known as Rooster, but my woman couldn't say it, so she calls me Wooster. Kinda stuck!" He motioned to a bench by a table, "Sit, sit! I'll get the coffee."

Fox joined Sean and they sat on the bench by the table, watching as the man poured the cups full. He poured himself a cup, sat down, "Muh woman'll join us in a minute. So, you folks takin' the Oregon Trail west, are ye?"

"No, no we're not," said Sean, then motioning toward the poles and wire asked, "What's that all about?"

The man laughed, "That there's progress! Them's telegraph wires, and we've got us a telegraph station right'chere," he declared. "An' within the year, we're gonna be a stage station. There's gonna be a stage line come right thru hyar an' on to Fort Bridger an' beyond!" He slapped his leg, "Betcha never thought there'd be telegraph and stages way out chere, did'ja?"

With a glance to Fox, Sean answered, "No, I didn't." He looked around, seeing the cabins had been recently built, then looked back at the man. "You folks haven't been here through a winter, have you?"

"Oh no. We've just been here since spring, but with the stage an' ever'thing, we figger this'll be a right proper town 'fore ya' know it! We're callin' it South Pass City!"

Sean looked to the west at the high rising hills, bluffs and the mountains to the north. This was country that was usually buried in deep snow almost all winter long, and he looked at the cabins, picturing them under six to ten feet of snow, drifts and more. He shook his head, "I hope you're plannin' on layin' in a lot of firewood. This country gets buried come winter time."

The man frowned, looked at Sean, "You been here in the winter?"

"That's right. And I'll be here this winter, only we'll be back that way," nodding his heads to the tail end of the Wind River Mountains, "and we'll be protected from the winds that'll blow the snow over the top of your cabins and not let you out till spring!"

Sean stood, "By the way, my name's Sean Saint, this is my wife, White Fox. Up on top of those hills yonder, there's a trail that cuts the timber goin' north. Our cabin is about two days ride from here along that trail, next to a big lake in the bottom. This ain't an invitation, but you know where we are if we're needed."

As Sean and Fox were mounting, Wooster's wife stepped out of the cabin, wiping her hands on her apron then shielding her eyes as she watched the two mount up. She didn't speak but waved her hand at Fox and Fox smiled back. Wooster said, "That's good to know. And if you ever need to send a telegram or a letter, we're also a mail drop, leastways we will be when the stage comes through. Nice meetin' ya' neighbor!"

SEAN WAS anxious and didn't sleep well that night. Rising early, they greeted the day from horseback as they pushed into the timber to follow the trail to the cabin. When they crested the last rise and the lake was visible through the trees, Sean reined up, twisted in his saddle and looked at Fox. She looked from him to the sapphire blue gem lying in the tall timber and smiled. "It is beautiful!" Sean smiled, gigged Dusty forward and in a short while they rode into the clearing by the cabin.

Once the horses were in the corral behind the cabin and stripped of their gear, the two newlyweds entered the cabin. It was surprisingly clean, and a scribbled note lay on the table. Sean read *We knew you would be back soon, so Red Hawk thought we oughta fix things up a little. We stayed here for some time, but she wanted to go back to her people. The horses are doin' fine in the upper pasture. You know where we are.*

Whiskers

Sean grinned as he remembered the big man and his wife. They had been great friends for several years and often took care of the cabin and horses if they had to leave. Sean explained to Fox and she smiled, "But now this is our home?"

"Yes, it is. Well, it's actually the home of my pa and ma, but I don't know if they're comin' back or not. But for now, it is our home!"

She smiled and drew near, lifting her arms around his neck she pulled him down for a kiss and said, "I am happy, boyfriend."

WATCH FOR: WINTER'S WAIF

THE NEXT INSTALLMENT IN THE ROCKY MOUNTAIN SAINT SERIES BY B.N. RUNDELL, COMING SOON.

ABOUT THE AUTHOR

Born and raised in Colorado into a family of ranchers and cowboys, B.N. Rundell is the youngest of seven sons. Juggling bull riding, skiing, and high school, graduation was a launching pad for a hitch in the Army Paratroopers. After the army, he finished his college education in Springfield, MO, and together with his wife and growing family, entered the ministry as a Baptist preacher.

Together, B.N. and Dawn raised four girls that are now married and have made them proud grandparents. With many years as a successful pastor and educator, he retired from the ministry and followed in the footsteps of his entrepreneurial father and started a successful insurance agency, which is now in the hands of his trusted nephew. He has also been a successful audiobook narrator and has recorded many books for several award-winning authors. Now finally realizing his life-long dream, B.N. has turned his efforts to writing a variety of books, from children's picture books and young adult adventure books, to the historical fiction and western genres

https://wolfpackpublishing.com/b-n-rundell/

Made in the USA
Coppell, TX
27 April 2023

16055069R00152